Florence Marryat

How they Loved him

Vol. II

Florence Marryat

How they Loved him
Vol. II

ISBN/EAN: 9783337047832

Printed in Europe, USA, Canada, Australia, Japan

Cover: Foto ©Andreas Hilbeck / pixelio.de

More available books at **www.hansebooks.com**

BY

FLORENCE MARRYAT
(Mrs Francis Lean).

IN THREE VOLUMES.

VOL. II.

LONDON: F. V. WHITE & CO.,
31 SOUTHAMPTON STREET, STRAND, W.C.

1882.

THE POPULAR NEW NOVELS AT ALL LIBRARIES.

THREE FAIR DAUGHTERS. By Laurence Brooke, Author of 'The Queen of Two Worlds,' etc.   3 vols.

SWEETHEART AND WIFE.   By Lady Constance Howard.   3 vols.

MY LADY CLARE.   By Mrs Eiloart, Author of 'How He Won Her,' etc.   3 vols.

'"My Lady Clare" is a pleasant, readable novel.'—*John Bull.*

'The interest is maintained with undeniable force and skill.'— *Daily Telegraph.*

A LOVELESS SACRIFICE.   By Ina L. Cassilis. Author of 'Guilty without Crime,' etc.   3 vols.

John Bull says :—'The story is a pleasant one—healthy in tone, lofty in teaching, and very sympathetic in manner and style.'

COLSTON AND SON, PRINTERS, EDINBURGH.

CONTENTS.

CHAPTER VI.

CHAPTER VII.

CHAPTER VIII.

HOW THEY LOVED HIM.

———◆———

CHAPTER I.

FOR EVER.

'It is the same together or apart,
  From life's commencement to its slow decline :
  We are entwined ; let death come slow or fast,
  The tie which bound the first endures the last.'

Byron.

T O describe the feelings of Fenella
Barrington at this period would
be almost impossible.   Not because no one has ever felt so deeply as
she did, but because such thoughts are not
to be adequately portrayed in black and

white. Arraigned before the judgment of the world, they would appear foolish, romantic, overstrained, and perhaps culpable ; to each individual heart alone, according to the circumstances under which they found it, must they answer for the consequences. Fenella's heart was in an exceptional condition when the passion of love overtook and conquered it. In the first place, she was very young ; and youth, like charity, ' believeth all things and hopeth all things.' She was too ignorant of human nature to doubt its truth—too ignorant of life to distrust its possibilities. And in the second place, she was very lonely and unhappy. She had no watchful parent to shield her innocence ; she had not even any one to call her to account for her actions. She was free as the air, unguarded as the birds that flew in it, unloved as the most friendless waif that was ever forsaken by its natural protectors.

Disappointed and alone ! What girl

under such circumstances could be expected not to answer with the whole strength of her nature to the call of love? Her heart was so empty of affection—it yearned so for it—that it would not have been strange had she succumbed to the appeal of any fellow-creature who desired to show her kindness—least of all to that of Geoffrey Doyne. For there was a fascination about him that was far above any physical attractions he may have possessed—a fascination which every woman felt who crossed his path, and many were left to rue. His tender eyes, and sensitive mouth, and dreamy poetical nature made him appear the most sympathetic and warm-hearted of human creatures; as indeed he was—whilst the humour lasted. But there were two formidable foes in his breast to war against his better feelings, and usually to overcome them, and these were a want of moral courage and a great love of self.

Geoffrey Doyne generally wanted to do

right, and, as a rule, he generally did wrong. His head told him the proper thing to do, but his heart failed him at the very moment he called upon it for support and courage. So he was the worst possible guide that could have been found for a young and susceptible girl who loved him ardently.

Fenella would have proved far the most trustworthy of the two. Her innocence made her the better fitted to lead the way, had she not loved him so blindly as to be incapable of believing him to be in the wrong.

The reverend mother had said of her to Eliza Bennett, 'She possesses the most dangerous attributes with which a young girl can encounter the world,—a heart so large and warm and generous, that where it loves it cannot see a fault, and a strong resolute nature that will act on its own impulses against all conventionality or advice.' And the reverend mother was right. Fenella was that most

dangerous combination — a child in ex-
perience, and a woman in feeling. In her
eyes Geoffrey Doyne was simply perfec-
tion ; and from the day he said he loved
her, she yielded herself up to his control
in everything. She looked on him rather
as a god than a man. She could not
understand how it was that so perfect a
creature condescended to dwell amongst
ordinary mortals. The air he breathed,
the flower he touched, the ground he
trod on became sacred to her from mere
contact with him. Hers was not the
frivolous, giggling, open-mouthed admiration of a school-girl ; it was the silent,
awe-struck adoration of a woman! She
would sit for hours absorbed in the contemplation of his features. Each move-
ment of his supple figure was a poem to
her, each tone of his voice a melody, each
glance from his eyes a dream of heaven.
She hung upon his words as if they had
been inspired ; and his touch, however
careless, had the power to thrill her with

a pleasure that was next door to pain.
A few days of intimate communion, of
mutually - confessed and openly - avowed
passion, made Geoffrey Doyne her ruler
—her inspiration—her very life.

And he knew it but too soon. He saw
that the girl had become his slave—
morally and physically ; that he had but
to lift his little finger to command her
obedience ; that with a glance of his eye
he could direct her actions or sway her
mind. And he loved her for it in return.
Let him have justice done him at this, the
fairest portion of his life. There is no
question that *he loved her!* Although he
was not sufficiently heroic, nor high-
minded, nor courageous to rank her
purity and child-like trust in him above
his own selfish gratification—although his
religion was not potent enough to gain the
mastery over the more natural religion of
love—still *he loved her!* Fenella was the
first woman who had ever touched his
heart, as he was the first man who had

ever attempted to win hers. Her face
was not more charming, perhaps, than
many he had met with before ; her talents
(if of a high order) were crude and unde-
veloped ; her love for himself, though
deep and glowing, was no more than he
had a right to expect from the other sex.
But she was the first whom he had ever
loved ; and there is a magic charm in
those words, *the first.* The first kiss, the
first woman, the first child, the first disappointment, the first death! Can any
future joy or sorrow equal these ? They
are events that stand alone in our lives :
they can never be repeated ; once gone,
they are gone for ever! In all the rest of
his life, though Geoffrey Doyne might love
a dozen other women, and swear a thousand
oaths of fidelity to them, he would never
love *in the same way* he loved Fenella
Barrington. More, he would never feel
the passion of love in his breast, even
though it burned ten times as strongly as
it burned for her, without giving one short,

quick sob of remembrance to the girl who
gave him her whole heart, and placed her
very life in his hands, upon the sands of
Ines-cedwyn! And if he could forget—
if his mortal nature proved so weak—
Heaven is still above us all, watching,
noting, jotting down on tablets of stone
each crime we commit against the heart
of a fellow-creature, to hold them up
before our eyes to all eternity. The time
will come when we shall be unable to
forget!

After the day on which they discovered
their mutual affection, Fenella Barrington
and Geoffrey Doyne met, if possible, more
frequently than they had done before.
Each morning found them on the sands
together, or if the young man pleaded
an unwelcome engagement with his sisters, it was only to impress upon Fenella
the double obligation of meeting him
when the evening shadows should have
fallen on the landslip. Ah! those dangerous moments spent beneath the soft

veil of dusk—when they sat side by side upon the golden sands, and watched the stars come out upon the summer sky, and their fresh, young voices rose up in unison to heaven in the thrilling notes of some love melody, or the more solemn tones of an evening hymn ; when their hands lay fast locked in one another's, and Fenella's head was pillowed on her lover's breast, till she heard no sound but the throbbing of his heart answering to her own. And they talked of the future—that glorious and apparently certain future, when they should always be together, and have no need to steal out, under cover of the evening, to meet each other on the sands.

It was provoking that, as yet, Geoffrey had been unable to write to Mrs Barrington and make a formal proposal for her daughter's hand, because but one letter had been received from that lady, dated from Genoa, and averring the intention of her party to move about for

a few weeks in the South before they
settled down in Mentone. But that was
of little consequence—so the lovers told
each other—because as soon as Mrs Barrington *was* settled, Geoffrey would go
over and see her, which would be far
better than writing—and they could not
be happier than they were.

It was now the end of June; two
months had slipped away in this sweet
courtship, and every day might bring
the letter to say that Fenella's mother
was settled at Mentone.

Eliza Bennett was up and about again.
She had even discarded the crutches with
which Dr Redfern had provided her, but
her leg was still stiff, and she had not yet
ventured to walk as far as the beach.
But some rumours had reached her ears
of the company in which her young mistress so constantly indulged. Of course
the boat and fishermen had seen the
courtship from the beginning. Tugwell,
who had so often to put up at the public

house, would have told them of it if they
had not had eyes to see it for themselves.
But it was nobody's business to carry the
news up to Benjamin Bennett's cottage.
If the young lady liked to amuse herself,
what was the odds to Ines-cedwyn? besides, Eliza Bennett was ailing, and there
was no need to worry her with a parcel of
tales about nothing. So the men told
the women to hold their tongues, and
consequently it was some time before
anybody spoke of Fenella's doings out
of their own circle.

But when Eliza Bennett had so far
recovered as to be in the garden, and
Martha had more time for gossiping with
her neighbours, they let their tongues
loose, and asked her to satisfy their
curiosity with regard to the handsome
stranger that came over to Ines-cedwyn
in his boat every day, and if he was going
to marry the young lady from the cottage
who sat for so many hours with him in
the Beach Bungalow. Of course it was

all news to Martha, and she ran open-mouthed with it to her sister-in-law.

'Only to think, 'Liza,' she exclaimed, 'what Winny Williams has just told me! Miss Fenella's got a beau, and such a fine lookin' feller too. They've bin meetin' each other at that there nasty ruined bungalow for weeks past, and having fine times, I warrant. Tugwell says the gentleman lives at Lynwern, but he's not sure as he's got his name properly. Only to think of your young lady! Well, sooner or later they all does it.'

Eliza Bennett was at first incredulous.

'I don't believe it,' she replied; 'the Ines-cedwyn folk must talk of something. I daresay Miss Fenella may have exchanged a word or two with the gentleman on the sands; but as for havin' a *beau*, why, Martha, she's that innercent, she don't know what it means! She'd run away more likely if any one were to say more than "good-day" to

her. You don't know my young lady;
she's the biggest child of her age I
ever saw.'

'Is she, now?' replied Martha meditatively. 'Well, I should have said the
same myself when she first come here;
but d'ye know, 'Liza, she's a deal changed
lately—more fidgety like, and don't eat
hearty, and allays a-jumpin' up and down
from her seat, with her colour comin' and
goin' like a flame o' fire. Ben ain't
very far seein' as a rule, but he told me
only last week as he thought there was
somethin' up with her.'

'Why didn't you tell me before?'
exclaimed her sister-in-law, in evident
distress.

'Why! what would ha' been the good
o' that—a' worryin' you for nothin' when
you're ill?'

'But I'd have spoken to Miss Fenella,
and found out the truth of it, Martha.
For she's one of the best young ladies
you ever see; she's like a lamb for obe-

dience, and I'm sure she'd no more go to
do the thing that is wrong than she'd fly!'

'Who said she had?' cried Martha.
'Lor' bless my heart, 'Liza! leave the
poor child alone. If she *is* having a bit
of fun with the young feller, what harm?
There's little enough to amuse her down
here, I'm sure, and she'll be all the better
for it. You wouldn't go and spoil her
game by makin' a fuss over it, would
you?'

'No; not if there's no harm, Martha;
certainly not! but, you see, Miss Fenella's
very young and easily led, and there's
no knowing what a gentleman might
get to say to her, seeing she's so pretty,
I must say I do distrust 'em, one and
all; and my mistress would never forgive me if any harm came to the young
lady.'

'Lor', 'Liza! how you do run on,' said
Martha. 'I shall be sorry I said anything about it next. Ain't a pretty girl
like that never to have a sweetheart? and

what harm do you think could come to
her with a real gentleman? He'll only
tell her a few lies, and she'll be none
the worse for 'em; so don't you go and
fret over it now, or you'll make yourself
ill again.'

Eliza promised she would not; but she
could not dismiss the subject from her
mind, for her dread of Mrs Barrington's
possible anger made her imagine all sorts
of danger to the girl under her charge.

'If it hadn't been for this stupid leg,'
she thought to herself, 'I'd have been
everywhere with Miss Fenella, and no
one couldn't have spoken to her without
my knowledge. And now Martha comes
to speak of it, there has been a great
change in her lately. She's more excited and forgetful like; and sometimes
she's as gay as a lark, and at others I've
seen her staring up at the sky with the
tears on her face, and yet with a smile
on her mouth. There's something very
strange about it all. How can I have

been so stupid as not to see it before!
But this leg has put everything else clean
out of my head.'

It was past nine o'clock when this
conversation took place, and Fenella had
gone down to the beach as usual, about
an hour before. Under the new point of
view from which she now regarded her
young lady's wanderings, Eliza Bennett
grew fidgety at her absence.

'I wonder what she's about this
evening?' she thought presently. 'It's
too dark to see anything on the
beach at this time o' night, and Miss
Fenella must know that supper's ready
and waiting for her. I wonder if
I could manage to get as far as the
bungalow. I've a good mind to try; and
I sha'n't feel easy now if I don't look a
bit more after her.'

Martha had gone to assist her husband
in the cowyard, and there was no one
to combat Eliza's desire, or tell her it
was foolish to attempt to do so much.

So she put on her bonnet and shawl, and taking a stick in her hand, commenced to hobble slowly in the direction of the beach.

Meanwhile Fenella and Geoffrey stood together in one of the rooms of the ruined villa. They were looking serious, but scarcely sad. Hope and trust were too strong in them for sadness.

'Oh, Geoffrey,' Fenella was saying, 'is it true? Must you really go?'

'I am afraid I must, my darling. I have received a most imperative letter from my brother Michael (that's the lawyer, you know, Fenella), urging me to go up to town and see him at once, on the most important business. I can't imagine what it is—something to do with money, I suppose. I don't think Michael would call anything else "important;" but, any way, I must go, and I shall start to-morrow morning.'

'And when will you be back, Geoffrey?'

'As soon as ever I can, my darling; you may rest assured of that. And meanwhile,

I shall write to you every day. What will old Bennett say when she sees the letters?'

'Never mind Bennett! She may be surprised, but she will not attempt to interfere with them. She is only my servant, Geoffrey. You do not suppose I would allow her to come between you and me?'

'Dear me! What an independent young woman you have grown! Who would imagine this was the same little girl that blushed scarlet each time I looked at her but two short months ago?'

'You have made me a woman,' said the girl with one of the scarlet blushes he alluded to. 'I feel now as if I should have courage to stand up against the whole world if it attempted to come between me and the love you bear me.'

'You shall never be put to the test, my Fenella. Nothing shall ever divide our love. I wish to goodness that letter would come from your mother, and then the matter would be settled.'

'And if—if she should be angry, and

refuse her consent to our marriage?'
faltered the girl.

'Then we are to be married without
her consent—is it not so? Why, Fenella! do you think any earthly power
could divide us now?'

She clung to him with a force that was
almost painful.

'Oh no, no! how could it? But, Geoffrey,
I wish—oh, how I wish!—that we could have
been married before you went to London.'

'My sweetheart, so do I. There is
nothing I long for more than the day
when we shall go to church and do all
that dreadful "swearing" you are so afraid
of. Only, I am afraid it must not be in
Lynwern. It would not be fair to you,
nor your mother, nor any one, Fenella.
Let me write to her first, darling; it cannot
be long now before you hear again; and
then if she raises any objection (which I
think most unlikely), I shall not hesitate a
moment to carry you straight off before
her eyes and marry you in the first church

we come to.   So be patient, my love, and
trust to me, and all will be right by-and-by.'

'And nothing—*nothing* shall ever divide
us?' she repeated, still clinging to him.

'Nothing, *so help me, God!*' he answered.   And that oath was registered in
heaven, and remains there to this day.

They sat together on one of the window-
sills for some time longer, with their arms
interlaced and their heads close together,
talking such sweet nonsense as the world
laughs at because it has no heart to
understand, but which makes up the sum
of happiness in this mortal life.

'And what am I to send my darling
from London?' demanded Geoffrey.   'In
all this time I have not given you one
present, because there was nothing worthy
of you in Lynwern ; but now you must
have something to remind you of your
lover.   What shall it be, sweetheart ?—a
locket or a ring ?'

'I don't want anything,' she said bash-
fully, 'but *you.*'

'Oh, you've got me fast enough, my child,' he answered, laughing; 'but come now, answer my question. Will you have a ring?'

She shook her head.

'No; not till you give me *that one*, Geoffrey.'

'That won't be long first, my darling! You'll be wanting to get it off again twelve months afterwards—you'll be so sick of it and me.'

'Don't—*don't!*' she murmured, as if smitten by a sudden pain.

'May I send you a locket, then, Mrs Doyne?' he continued playfully, for he saw her spirits were sinking; 'a great big gold locket to put your husband's hair in, and sleep with under your pillow every night until you see him again—for I know that is what you silly girls do when you've got a lover.'

At this proposal her face brightened.

'Yes; I should like to have a locket —very, *very* much, dear Geoffrey; and

I will wear it as long as ever I live.'

Then he rose suddenly, and said that he must go.

' Past ten o'clock, I declare, my dearest, and I have to be up at eight. God bless you, my Fenella! God keep you for me! Oh, this parting is an awful wrench, though it is but for so short a time.'

The girl did not say much, but her face went suddenly as white as a sheet, and she clung to him as though her arms would never be unlocked again.

' You will come back soon ?' she whispered, trembling like a leaf.

' Very, very soon—in a week at latest— most likely in a couple of days. Don't shake so, my darling! remember we are pledged to each other for life. Surely, Fenella, you have not one doubt of me ?'

' *I trust you as I trust God*,' she answered solemnly. They were her last words—their farewells had been exchanged already ; in another moment he had broken

from her clasp, and was gone. Fenella
watched him as he strode across the sands
and pushed off in the little boat that was
waiting for him. She kissed her hand in
the moonlight again and again, but he was
too far off to see the signal; then, with a
sound that was half a sob and half a sigh,
she turned away. As she did so she saw
something glittering on the dusty floor—
something lying in a streak of moonlight
shone like a diamond beneath her feet.
It was one of Geoffrey's sleeve-links that
had fallen from his cuff as he embraced
her—a twisted thing of enamel and gold
that Fenella had often noticed on his
wrist before. With a cry of joy she
pounced upon it, and hid it in her bosom.
She did not know till that moment how
much she could prize anything that had
been his; she could not realise how bitter
separation between those who love, can be,
till she had tasted it. As she prepared to
return to the cottage, a dark figure in the
doorway of the bungalow made her start.

'Bennett!' she exclaimed, in the same moment, 'is that you? Oh, how you frightened me! I never supposed for a moment you could get down so far. But how you are shaking! I am sure it has been too much for you.'

'Miss Fenella,' said the servant, as she sat down on the verandah floor to recover herself, 'I came to see after you, my dear! Do you know as it's past ten o'clock, and the supper's been on the table this hour and more? It's too late for a young lady to be out by herself, and in such a lonely place as Ines-cedwyn.'

'Why, nurse, I thought its loneliness was the very thing that made it safe. This is not the first evening I have been on the sands till ten o'clock, and Martha never spoke to me on the subject, or told me I was wrong.'

'No, Miss Fenella; 'tisn't Martha's business to speak to you; and I've been in bed, you see, and knew nothin' about it; but I'm afraid as your mamma wouldn't

think it was right. And—if I may make
so bold, miss—who was that gentleman
who parted with you just as I came up
to the back of the house ? '

Fenella was startled by the question,
but she was too proud to attempt to deny
the truth.

' That was a friend of mine, Bennett—a
gentleman who often comes over to Ines-
cedwyn. You need not worry yourself
about him. It is all right, and mamma
will say so, too, as soon as she hears it.'

' Is he a friend of your mamma's, miss ? '

' Yes ; that is, he doesn't know her yet,
but he soon will. He is the friend of all
of us, nurse—the very best friend we ever
had.'

' I am glad of that, my dear ; but I hope
he won't come here again till he's seen
your mamma. Because it isn't quite the
proper thing, you know, for a gentleman to
meet a young lady so often, and at all sorts
of odd times. It makes people talk, Miss
Fenella, and that's not good for any one.'

What was it in the girl's face that made the servant half afraid of saying even as much as she did ? A new light, a new dignity, something she had never seen there before, seemed to settle on Fenella's brow, and relegate Eliza Bennett to her proper position. She could not speak to her young mistress now as she had done on the journey from Calais to Dover.

'Bennett,' said the girl presently, 'I daresay it may seem strange to you, because you do not understand; neither can I give you any explanation till I have seen my mother. But you may make your mind easy on one score—the gentleman has gone away, for the present. He will not be back again, most probably, until we have heard from Mentone; and then everything will be right. And now, let me take you home, dear nurse. I wish you hadn't come down here after me; I am so afraid you may have hurt yourself. There! lean on my arm as hard as ever you like; you cannot tire me; and we will go home to-

gether.   And, please, don't speak to me
again about the—I mean, about the subject
you mentioned just now, because I can
say nothing until I have seen mamma, and
then you will understand that all your fears
are groundless.   Lean harder, dear nurse ;
that is right.   I am strong enough to bear
your weight and my own too.'

CHAPTER II.

IN A STRAIT.

'Men have many loves; their true names are—or Vice
or Vanity, or Feebleness or Folly.'—*Ariadne*.

GEOFFREY DOYNE had but
spoken the truth when he said
that his brother's letter was a
most imperative one. It had contained
as sharp a summons as it was possible to
send a man :—

'Come up to London as soon as ever
you receive this,' it ran. 'I must see you
at once, and on business of the utmost
importance.'

The brothers had inherited money at
the death of their mother, which was in-
vested in stock, and under the management

of Michael Doyne, and Geoffrey naturally
thought that his presence was needed on
account of some selling-out or buying-
in. His brother did not seem to him to
have a soul above money. He could
not imagine his troubling himself on
any other matter.

He went up to town by an early train
the following day, and the same idea was
in his mind as he entered the lawyer's
office.

'What's up now?' he said, as he encountered Michael's portentous counten-
ance. 'Have Persians fallen, or Hudson's
Bay gone up? I do wish you could
manage these matters without my inter-
ference, Michael. You know how I detest
business, and how perfectly I am satisfied
that you know a great deal more about
it than I do.'

'But this is unfortunately a matter
which I could not settle on my own
authority,' replied his brother gravely.
'Come into the inner office, Geoffrey. I

cannot speak to you unless we are perfectly alone.'

'This looks ominous,' cried Geoffrey gaily, as he ensconced himself in an armchair and flicked the dust off his dainty boots.

'It is ominous,' replied the other, 'and I trust you are not going to make a jest of it. It is likely to cause trouble enough before long, unless I can bring you to reason.'

'What are you driving at?' said Geoffrey.

'Simply this—that Dr Robertson called at my office yesterday morning and gave me a piece of information that horrified me.'

The younger brother changed colour.

'Well, go on,' he said carelessly; 'what had the old gentleman to say for himself?'

'You know, Geoffrey, as well as I do. He came to tell me that you had broken off your engagement with his daughter Jessie.'

'It is not true; it was Jessie who broke off her engagement with me.'

'I cannot believe it, Geoffrey. Dr Robertson came to me in the greatest distress. He said that both he and his wife had observed that their daughter was out of health and spirits for some weeks past, but that they had not connected the circumstance with your engagement until they noticed that all correspondence had ceased between you. Then they questioned Jessie, and the truth came out—that you had written to her some time back, and said you didn't care for her.'

'Not exactly that,' replied Geoffrey; 'but I told her I did not care for her as I ought to do for the woman I was going to make my wife; and that's the truth, Michael. I *don't* care for her, and I never shall; and under the circumstances, it would be perfectly absurd my marrying her!'

'You should have thought of that before you proposed to her,' remarked Michael drily.

' I did ; but I was drawn into it. You know I was as thoroughly "hooked" by the old woman as ever a man could be.'

' Perhaps you were—that is your own business ; but having been "hooked," as you call it, you must submit to be "landed." '

' Do you mean to say, then, that you consider I am bound to marry Jessie Robertson ? '

' I do, most decidedly.'

' What ! after she has sent me back my letters and presents ? '

' That has nothing to do with it, Geoffrey. The poor girl sent them back because she was ignorant how else to act. Had she consulted her parents, they would not have permitted her to do so. Jessie would set you free as it is ; but Dr and Mrs Robertson are quite of a different opinion. They won't let you off so easily.'

' They intend to keep me to my word ? '

' I am afraid there is no doubt of it. The doctor might be talked over, but you know what his wife is. He says she is furious, and declares that, if you refuse to keep to your engagement with Jessie, she will sue you for a breach of promise; and that's a sort of thing our family could not allow, you know, Geoffrey.'

The younger man sat silent and sullen, with a face of the deepest perplexity.

' I *must* get out of it somehow,' he said presently. 'You are cleverer than I am, Michael; can't you help me?'

' I don't see my way to it, Geoffrey. You proposed to the girl of your own accord, and the engagement has been made public. What earthly excuse can you have for getting out of it?'

' Why, that I don't love her, and that I won't marry her. No; by George! I won't, if I hang for it!'

' There's another woman in the case,' remarked his brother casually.

' Yes, there is,' said Geoffrey.

' Some girl at Ines-cedwyn?'

' Who told you that?'

'I heard of it when I was down at
Lynwern. Well, I daresay it will be hard
lines, Geoffrey; but you must give her
up. You can't marry them both.'

'I won't marry Jessie Robertson,' said
Geoffrey stoutly.

'You *must*, man—you *must!* Don't
talk nonsense; try to look at the matter
in a reasonable light. After all, it's only
a toss-up between them, and why should
one girl suffer more than the other?
There are certain social laws, you know,
Geoffrey, which we cannot break with
impunity, and this is one of them. Your
honour is concerned in your keeping your
engagement, and you cannot cancel it
without disgracing the whole family. For
our sakes, therefore (if not for your own),
you must do the right thing by Jessie
Robertson.'

'My honour may be concerned elsewhere as well,' rejoined Geoffrey, in a
somewhat lowered voice, 'and my happiness as well as my honour. Michael, I

will pay any forfeit, or incur any penalty they may choose to put upon me; but I cannot, and I will not, marry Jessie. I will cut my throat first.'

'No, don't do that,' said his brother, as if he had proposed a thing of every-day occurrence. 'I don't approve of marriage myself as a rule, but I think of the two courses it would be the preferable one to pursue. Little Jessie isn't half bad, you know, when you come to think of it; and if you would only believe me, my dear fellow,' he continued, as he laid his hand on his brother's shoulder, 'one woman will be just the same to you as another when you have been married for three months.'

'Ah! that's what *you* think of it,' said Geoffrey; 'it shows how much you know of the matter.'

'Is this young lady at Ines-cedwyn, then, so very handsome?'

'No.'

'Clever?'

' Not particularly so.'

' Rich ?'

' Certainly not.'

' Then what's the great attraction in her, that you should wish to break the heart of a good little girl like Jessie Robertson for her sake ?'

' It is one that I don't think you'd understand, Michael,—*I love her!*'

The lawyer laughed.

' My dear boy, I've heard you say the same thing so often before. Excuse me if I think you could manage that (if you tried) with any one of the sex.'

' At any rate, I don't intend to try it with Jessie Robertson.'

Michael Doyne looked grave ; he did not like this determined refusal on the part of his brother. It looked so much as if (for once) Geoffrey were in earnest.

' Well, look here!' he said suddenly ; ' if you really want to get out of this scrape, Geoffrey, you can only do it by persuading the old people to let you off. Suppose you

meet me at the Robertsons' this evening to
talk the matter over ? Will you do so ?'

' I shall tell them the truth,' said Geoffrey. ' I shall tell them I'm in love with
somebody else, and they must think what
they like of it.'

' Perhaps that will be the best plan, after
all,' replied his brother ; ' but, at any rate,
you must see them. It was only by pro-
mising to summon you to London that I
dissuaded the old man from following you
to Lynwern.'

' Was it so bad as that ?' asked Geoffrey,
startled.

' It was, indeed! They're in a rare
state in Blenheim Square, I can tell you,
and would have written straight off to the
pater if I had not promised a lot of things
in your name, which I trust you will be
found ready to fulfil. I hardly know how
the pater would take this, Geoffrey. The
Robertsons are his oldest friends, as you
know ; and he would be quick to resent
an affront to them. I'm not sure but

what it might militate against your future prospects!'

'I can't help it if it does,' said Geoffrey, with a sigh. 'I am not going to blast all my happiness for life to please anybody.'

'Ah! that's only talking,' replied his brother carelessly, as he bid him good-bye, and told him not to fail to keep his appointment in Blenheim Square at nine o'clock.

Geoffrey strolled towards his club, ill at ease. He did not waver for a moment from his determination, but he was afraid he might have trouble in keeping to it. He would have had little fear of being able to make Dr Robertson see the matter in a sensible light, but the doctor was unfortunately a cipher in his own house, where Mrs Robertson reigned supreme; and Geoffrey (in common with the rest of mankind) stood terribly in awe of her.

He tried to divert his thoughts and while away the time by purchasing the promised

locket for Fenella—a gold locket with a
wreath of laurel on it in blue enamel —(was
it prophetic of her future destiny ?)—surrounding the emblems of Love and Faith
and Hope. Geoffrey thought the design
a pretty one, and bought the trinket on
the spot. Fenella would think of him
when she saw the laurel—the laurel which
grows to adorn the head of heroes ; and
the cross and heart and anchor were
emblematic of her own feelings—feelings
which he had called God to witness should
never be wounded through his means.

It was something to do to buy the locket,
and have a piece of his hair put in it, and
see it packed and addressed to Ines-cedwyn,
and to picture the innocent delight of the
receiver when it reached her hands the
following morning. But still hours inter-
vened before he could set off to keep his
appointment in Blenheim Square, and the
men who met him at his club, and 'chaffed'
him on keeping out of town at the best
season of the year, could not imagine what

had come to Geoffrey Doyne—he was so
distrait and peevish, not to say rude, in
the irritation caused by his perplexity and
doubt. When at last he reached the house,
Michael was ready to receive him in the
hall.

'I thought it better for me to come here
first, and smooth matters over a little,' he
said as his brother entered.

'I almost wish now that I had written
instead,' replied Geoffrey. 'However, I
am sure that Dr Robertson is too sensible
not to understand my motives.'

'I am afraid the doctor is out,' said
Michael Doyne. 'However, you will see
Mrs Robertson, and it is all the same
thing.'

He knew it was not the same thing,
and so did his brother, but it was too
late for remonstrance. Geoffrey was
already on the threshold of the library,
where Mrs Robertson sat in state to
receive him.

To say that this lady was a con-

glomeration of all the most ferocious
mothers - in - law that ever existed, is not
to say too much. Her sharp tongue and
vixenish temper were well known in the
circle of her acquaintance, and she joined
them to an obstinacy that was unequalled.
It was she alone who had insisted upon
Geoffrey Doyne being brought to book
for his defalcation, and forced to fulfil
his promises to her daughter. Good old
Dr Robertson might have shaken his
head over his faithlessness to his dying
day, but he would never have dreamt
of insisting that he should marry the girl;
and Jessie herself, although she inherited
somewhat of her mother's spirit, was too
young to have made such good use of
it. But Mrs Robertson was above such
petty scruples. Jessie was one of seven
daughters, and this young man, who had
the most excellent prospects, had formally entered into an engagement to
marry her, and now wanted to back out
of it, and her mother was determined to

know the reason why. So she sat, en-
throned in her husband's arm-chair, ready
to receive the culprit—her sandy hair
drawn tightly off her forehead, as though
to say she would admit of no com-
promise, and her hard steel-grey eyes
fixed on him with the look of an in-
quisitor.

Geoffrey Doyne, though with some
hesitation, advanced in the old way, and
held out his hand.

'No, thank you, Mr Doyne,' she said
tartly; 'not until this most unpleasant
business is settled between us. Be good
enough to seat yourself. I am glad your
brother is here to be witness to what
passes at our interview.'

Geoffrey flushed to the temples, but he
did as she desired him.

'My brother is here as my friend, Mrs
Robertson,' he replied. 'Otherwise he
can have no possible concern in my private affairs.'

'I don't know that, Mr Doyne,' said

his hostess. 'Did you come here as *our friend*, it might be so ; but under the circumstances, I should think very few *gentlemen* would be found willing to take your side.'

'Do you mean to insinuate, madam—' commenced Geoffrey hotly ; but Michael came between them as mediator.

'Mrs Robertson,' he said, 'I persuaded my brother to come here to-night that we might have an explanation, not a quarrel ; and I do not see how re-crimination can help the cause on either side. Will you hear what he has to say in extenuation of his conduct, or would you prefer to be the first to speak ? '

'I wish to say first what I think of him,' replied Mrs Robertson.

'Let it be so, then. Geoffrey, you see the justice of this. Mrs Robertson is not only a lady and your hostess, but she stands in the position of the injured party. Let me ask you, therefore, to listen patiently to whatever she may have to say, and you can justify your own action in the matter afterwards.'

'Which, I should imagine, Mr Geoffrey Doyne will find it most difficult to do,' interposed Mrs Robertson.

'No such thing, madam,' broke in Geoffrey warmly. 'I have the best possible excuse—'

But Michael came again to the rescue.

'Patience, my dear fellow—patience! You will never arrive at a satisfactory conclusion unless each consents to hear what the other has to say.'

Geoffrey sank into his chair again; and Mrs Robertson turned her back on him without ceremony.

'You will excuse me, Mr Doyne,' she said to the elder brother, 'if I prefer, for the present at all events, to address myself to you. The case stands simply thus. Last year Mr Geoffrey Doyne stayed for a month in our house, and I trusted him implicitly in the company of

all my daughters, with whom he appeared
on the best of terms—'

'Of course I was. I romped with
one as much as the other,' interposed
Geoffrey.

But Mrs Robertson took no notice of
the remark.

'After a while, however, I perceived
that he admired Jessie above the rest;
indeed, on several occasions I had seen
familiarities take place between them—'

'She used to come and sit on my
lap whether I would or no,' grumbled
Geoffrey.

'So I considered it my duty as a
mother,' continued the lady, waving her
hand, as though to wave the younger
brother off into infinitesimal space, 'to
ask him his intentions with regard to
her, and was greatly astonished to find
that he had no intentions whatever.'

'Of course I hadn't—never thought of
such a thing,' said Geoffrey.

'But you *ought* to have thought of it; it

was most reprehensible,' replied his brother, frowning.

'I am so glad you see it in *our* light, dear Mr Doyne,' rejoined Mrs Robertson; 'for it is hard, after so many years of friendly intercourse have subsisted between the families, to think of a rupture taking place now. The dear doctor feels it keenly. The suspense has quite aged him.'

'Oh, it must not be,' said Michael decidedly; and Geoffrey felt a chill run through him at the words.

'Of course I remonstrated with your brother,' resumed Mrs Robertson, 'as he will do me the justice to acknowledge, and pointed out to him the harm he had done our dear girl, and the misery he had caused her. And then Dr Robertson and his father both spoke to him; and the issue was, that he proposed formally to my husband for Jessie's hand (we have the letter now, Mr Doyne), and the engagement was ratified between them. Of course

our friends all know of it ; we never dreamt
for a moment that Mr Geoffrey Doyne
could be so *base* to go back from his
written word ; and the poor child has been
actually making the linen for her trousseau
for the last three months. When, the
other day, as I was questioning her on
her altered looks and spirits, she burst
into tears, and, to my *amazement*, told me
that it was all over between them ; that
Mr Geoffrey Doyne had sent for his letters
and presents to be returned to him, and
that he had been cruel enough to write and
tell the dear girl that he had never cared
for her, and that he refused to marry
her,—the basest, cruellest, most heartless
conduct I ever heard of in my life,' continued Mrs Robertson, trembling with
anger, ' and after the kindness and hospi-
tality he had received at our hands too !
But it cannot be allowed, Mr Doyne. I
will not sit by quietly and see my poor
child pine away in consequence of such
treachery. Your brother must fulfil the

engagement he entered into with her, or she shall have public compensation for his desertion. The world shall not have it in its power to say that we boasted idly of our daughter's expectations.'

'Am I to be allowed to speak now?' demanded Geoffrey, who had with difficulty kept quiet during the last part of this harangue.

'If Mrs Robertson has quite finished,' said his brother coldly.

'I have said all I wish to say,' replied the lady, 'and no explanations Mr Geoffrey Doyne can offer me in return can ever excuse his conduct to my daughter.'

'Perhaps not in *your* eyes, madam,' said Geoffrey; 'but you have appealed to the judgment of the world. I am glad you have done me the justice to acknowledge that I never had any intention of proposing to Jessie until you forced me to do so. And therein lies my greatest fault. I should have resisted your arguments

then as I do now. I have made the
task doubly hard by delay. Ever since
I yielded to your wishes in that respect,
I have seen how wrong I was to do so.
Each day has convinced me, more and
more, that I am not, and I never was,
in love with your daughter, and that if
I marry her we shall only make each
other miserable for life. It was with this
conviction that I wrote to her a month
ago—telling her the truth. I did not say
I would not marry her, neither did I
ask her to return my letters or presents.
I said just what I have told you—that
I had not considered sufficiently before I
made that proposal of marriage to her,
and that I did not care for her so much
as I ought to do. And if that is being
base and dishonourable in your eyes, it
is not in mine. I consider I should
have been much more to blame had I
married her without telling her the truth.'

'Unfortunately, you see, Geoffrey, it
is not what *you* think, but what the world

will say about the matter,' remarked
Michael gravely; 'and there is no doubt
that a thing of this kind militates against
a girl's prospects in life.'

'*Militates against her prospects!*' cried
Mrs Robertson shrilly; 'I should think
it did—it ruins them! Do you suppose
I am going to let my daughter be pointed
at as having been jilted—*and by you!*'
she ended, with withering scorn.

'Would you prefer her, then, to marry
a man who does not love her?' retorted
Geoffrey.

'That is of little consequence,' replied
the lady. '*No* men care for their wives
(as far as I can see) in the present day.
The mere fact of their *being* their wives
is sufficient to make them indifferent!
But my daughter is of a very different
disposition from you. She is amiable
and affectionate and loving, and I will
not see her heart broken and her future
prospects spoiled for any man alive.'

'If you knew all, Mrs Robertson,' resumed Geoffrey, colouring, 'you would see that you could not break her heart more readily than by marrying her to me.'

'You had better make a clean breast whilst you are about it,' suggested his brother.

'Perhaps you are right. Well, then, Mrs Robertson, my objection to renewing my engagement with Jessie does not lie wholly in the fact that I do not care sufficiently for her to make her a good husband. There is a stronger reason than that—a more insurmountable one. I am in love with another woman!'

He said the words slowly, as though they contained an argument to quench all her maternal hopes. But they had only the effect of making her more angry and determined.

'And do you call that an *excuse?*' she exclaimed; 'it is an aggravation of your offence. You are in love with another woman, and so *my* daughter is to go to the wall! My Jessie is to be deprived throughout life of all you had promised to give her, because you have taken it into your head to set up some one else in her stead. But you will find it is not quite so easy to chop and change in that manner, Mr Doyne. You have pledged your word to my daughter, and you must redeem it—or give her such compensation as the law may award her.'

'You will surely not bring this matter into court?' cried Geoffrey, with horror. 'You will never drag your daughter's name through the newspapers as the plaintiff in a breach of promise case?'

Mrs Robertson saw her advantage, and clung to it.

'We certainly *shall*,' she replied, ' unless you think better of the insult you have offered us. The doctor and I have talked this matter over, and he has left it entirely in my hands. He is no more disposed to sit by quietly, and see Jessie's heart broken without an effort to save her, than I am.'

'But how can you improve the affair by

making it public? You should consider
your daughter's feelings,' said the young
man, in evident distress. He did not perceive that the agitation he evinced was the
weakest card he could play into her hands;
nor did he guess that the threat she used
towards him had been suggested by his
astute lawyer brother.

'That is *our* business,' replied Mrs
Robertson coldly, 'and we shall do what
we consider best for our child without
any reference to her feelings. Neither
do I think *you* are the proper person to
remind me of my duty in that respect, Mr
Doyne, considering the *very little* regard
you have shown towards them yourself.'

'What *am* I to do?' demanded Geoffrey, in a low voice, of his brother.

'You'll have to stick to it, my boy. I
don't see any way out of it,' replied
Michael, in the same tone.

'I *cannot*—it is impossible. I will die
first,' said the younger man, in a voice of
despair.

'Well, Mr Doyne,' exclaimed Mrs Robertson after a short pause, 'is it of any use our prolonging this interview? Mr Geoffrey does not appear to be disposed to do what is right and honourable in the matter, and therefore it only remains for the doctor and myself to take the steps that seem best to us. And the first thing, I believe, my husband proposes to do is to go down and have an interview with your father at Ryelands.'

'Might I ask you, my dear Mrs Robertson, as a personal favour to myself,' said Michael Doyne, in his blandest voice, 'to allow Geoffrey a couple of days in which to think over what you have said to him? I feel convinced that, if you will do so, we shall have arrived at some satisfactory conclusion by that time. For my sake, Mrs Robertson—will you do it for *my* sake?'

'Well, Mr Doyne, for *your* sake I will; for I know we have your good wishes, although we appear to have lost those of

your brother. In a couple of days, then, I
shall expect to hear from you; and meanwhile I shall say nothing to my daughter,
nor take any more decided steps in the
matter. Good-night, dear Mr Doyne;
whatever happens, I shall always feel that
you have proved yourself a true and faithful friend to us,' and shaking hands with
the elder brother, Mrs Robertson swept
out of the room without vouchsafing one
glance towards the spot where Geoffrey
stood, silent and dejected.

'Come on, Geoff,' said Michael briskly,
as soon as she had disappeared; 'we
had better be going home; it is no use
our remaining longer here.'

The younger man followed him mecha-
nically to the hall door. His brain was
in such a whirl he hardly knew what he
was about.

'What *am* I to do?' he repeated, in a
confused manner, as they walked through
the square together.

'Well, to tell you the plain truth,

Geoffrey, I only see one thing for you to do, and that is to renew your engagement, and marry the girl, and take her back to India with you.'

'You forget the other,' said Geoffrey gloomily.

'No, I don't, my dear boy. I see the mess you're in as plainly as you do. But the other is a matter of *feeling*, Geoffrey, and this is a matter of *right*. Tell me a little about this young lady at Inescedwyn. Are her parents staying there?'

'No; she is with a servant.'

'You haven't said anything to them about marrying her, then?'

'Not yet.'

'It's only been a little spooning affair on your own account, eh?'

'Yes; I suppose you'd call it so.'

'Well, then, my dear Geoffrey, there's no question about the matter. You must break it off.'

'I *can't* do that, Michael.'

'You can, if you choose.'

' I *cannot.* There are reasons—'

' Oh yes! I understand all your reasons
before you tell me. You like her much
better than this one; in fact, you're
over head and ears in love with her,
and you want to marry her, and take
her out to India. That's it now, isn't
it? Well, I allow that it is very hard,
and, as I said before, I daresay it will
cut you up to have to part from her and
marry Jessie Robertson instead; but *it
must be done*, Geoffrey. There's the long
and the short of it. Your honour demands the sacrifice, and respect for your
family demands it. We can't have our
name dragged through a breach of
promise case, and connected with that
of the Robertsons. It would be too
disgraceful. I don't believe my father
would ever speak to you again. And
then, there's something to be said for
Jessie into the bargain. The girl's
awfully fond of you. The doctor says
she's so changed by your behaviour,

that you'd hardly know her; and I
don't see why she should be made to
suffer any more than the other one.
You can't keep your word to *both*, that's
clear; and Jessie Robertson will bear
the more open disgrace of the two, if
you break with her. Now, do go home
and try to think it over in that light.
Some one must bear the brunt of your
folly in any case; but if you persevere
in your present determination, we shall
all have to bear it, which isn't quite fair
upon us.'

Geoffrey did go home—miserable, undecided, and almost hopeless. Still, he
trusted that something might turn up
to help him out of his difficulty—that
Jessie's parents might relent, or the girl
herself refuse to renew their engagement.
Surely, he thought, if he told her to her
face he didn't love her, she would never
hold him to his word.

Meanwhile there was no reason that
his poor trusting Fenella should suffer

for his fault. Time enough for her to learn the worst when the worst came. So he sat down and wrote her a long loving letter (such as he knew she would carry in her bosom all the day), and told her he was afraid his business would detain him in town longer than he had expected ; but he did not mention what that business was. And when he had finished the letter, he laid his head down upon the paper and burst into tears.

'It is impossible,' he kept on repeating to himself. 'I *cannot*—I *must* not desert her. Not *now*—O God ! not *now*.'

His task would have been much easier if the other girl had not cared for him also, but he knew too well that she did care. It had been his flattered vanity at her evident affection that had drawn him into the noose that galled him now. Still he thought, if all other means failed, he must make an appeal to Jessie's generosity to set him free. He did not know that her temperament was of so jealous

a nature, that the very plea he urged
for liberty would be an incentive to her
to bind him closer. When the two days
of grace were over, he was as distracted
and undecided as ever, and Michael had
the greatest difficulty in persuading him
to put in an appearance in Blenheim
Square.

The meeting this time, however, was
of a more friendly character. Dr Robertson was present, and Michael Doyne had
already consulted with the parents on the
most politic step to be taken.

'We have no wish to appear harsh or
oppressive, my dear young friend,' commenced the doctor, who had been previously 'coached' by his wife what to say;
'but we have our child's happiness to
consult in this matter, and I am bound
to tell you that it is very seriously concerned. Mrs Robertson and I have, therefore, after mature deliberation, come to
the conclusion that Jessie is, after all,
the proper person to decide whether the

engagement shall continue or not, and we shall leave it entirely in her hands.'

Geoffrey's face flushed with hope.

' Do I understand you, sir, that Miss Robertson and I are to settle this busi-. ness by ourselves, and that you will abide by her decision, whatever it may be ? '

' Yes; that is our wish, Mr Doyne. After all, it is *her* happiness, and not *ours*, that is at stake; and if she tells us she has released you of her own free will, we shall take no further steps in the matter.'

' Thank you—thank you a thousand times,' said Geoffrey fervently. ' Does Jessie know I am in the house ? May I see her now ?'

' Yes; I have prepared my daughter for the interview,' replied Mrs Robertson, with a grim smile, as she preceded the young man out of the room.

Geoffrey followed her briskly, his heart throbbing with hope. He thought he should

have no difficulty in making Jessie understand how much better it would be for
both of them to be free.

Mrs Robertson led him to the drawing-
room and opened the door.

'Jessie, my dear,' she said quietly,
'here is Mr Geoffrey Doyne, who wishes
to speak to you.'

Then she retreated, and left the young
people together.

Now, until that morning Jessie Robertson had been entirely ignorant that she
had any rival to dispute her possession
of Geoffrey Doyne. She had accepted
his letter just as he wrote it, and had
never lost hope that he would find out
he had been mistaken, and return some
day and ask her to take back those
presents, and give him a place in her
affections once more. And she was quite
ready to do so, for, truth to say, he had
never lost that place. His handsome face
and figure had made an irrevocable im-
pression on her mind, and if she did not

love him with all the ardour of Fenella
Barrington, she loved him to the utmost
power of her nature—and no one can
do more. The rupture of their engagement had been a great shock to her, and
the disappointment had left its traces on
her features—had darkened the lines beneath her eyes, and washed the colour
from her rosy cheeks.

Mrs Robertson had seen all this ; she
knew that the girl looked pathetic and
pretty, and the young man was emotional
and easily impressed ; and she trusted a
great deal to the effect Jessie's altered
appearance would have upon him. Besides, she had, as she said, prepared her
daughter for this interview. She had
hinted at the possibility of some low-born
rival as a means of rousing the girl's
jealousy, and then she had implored her,
for the sake of Geoffrey Doyne's family
(no less than for his own), to be firm, and
bring him back to his allegiance. He
would thank her for it afterwards (the

mother said), when he knew his own heart better, and could rate her devotion for him at its true value. So Jessie came forward —rather timidly, it is true, but still very affectionately, and much in the old style, and lifted her tearful blue eyes to his face.

'I *knew* you would come back,' she murmured. 'I knew you would remember our old affection some day. Mamma said it was impossible that you could quite forget me.'

For a moment he almost forgot his mission in looking at her pale cheeks and attenuated figure.

'Why, Jessie,' he exclaimed, 'have you been ill?'

'Yes—a little. What does it matter? I fretted, of course—I could not help fretting; but I shall be all right again now.'

'Do you mean to say my letter caused this? Oh, what a brute I am!' cried Geoffrey.

'Don't say that,' replied Jessie softly, as

she sat down beside him. 'You did it for the best, I am sure.'

'I did indeed. I thought it would be less dishonourable to cancel our engagement than to let you marry me without knowing the truth. For I am not worthy of you, Jessie, and since we have been separated I have thought so much more seriously of such things. Marriage is a very solemn contract, is it not? And it would be unjust to let you enter into it with any one who does not love you as you deserve. Don't you agree with me?'

'But I always thought you loved me more than I deserved, Geoffrey,' she said, in a low voice; 'for, after all, what is there in me to love?'

'There is everything — everything to make a man happy, if he were not only too great a fool to appreciate it, Jessie.'

'But you made me quite happy,' she whispered.

'Did I? I am afraid I should not make you happy for long. I own an atrociously bad temper, Jessie—irritable and easily put out; and I am a selfish, heartless sort of fellow at the best. You would have wearied of me in no time, and then there would have been no remedy for either of us. It was better to put a stop to it before it was too late, wasn't it?'

'I should soon have grown used to your tempers, Geoffrey—all men have them, mamma says—and I never thought you heartless; at least, not until you sent me that letter.' And then she began to cry.

'Jessie, did that letter hurt you so very much?'

'Oh, terribly,' she said, amidst her sobs; 'how could it be otherwise when I had made up my mind we were to be married so soon, and half my things were made, too, and I had asked my cousins to be bridesmaids? And now—now it seems as if everything in the whole world was over for me, and I should never be happy again—never!'

'Oh, don't cry—for Heaven's sake, don't

cry!' said Geoffrey despairingly, 'and let me try and think what is best to be done.'

They sat silent for a few moments, whilst Jessie caught her breath, and dabbed her eyes with her pocket-hand-kerchief. Then Geoffrey said gravely,—

'Jessie! I thought—and I think still —that we shall never be happy as man and wife; but your father and mother consider that I have gone so far in proposing to you, that I have no right even to suggest such a thing as alter-ing our minds, and that it must rest with *you* to decide whether our mar-riage takes place or not.'

'I would much rather it took place,' sobbed the girl.

'Listen to me,' went on her com-panion, 'and don't decide in a hurry. Remember the whole happiness of our lives depends upon your answer. I am compelled to tell you—in justice to you and to myself—that I do not love you as I ought to do. In fact, Jessie, I—

I—(don't be angry with me for saying
it) — but   I — care   for somebody else;
and that fact alone   would make   my
marriage with you   a   sacrilege and   a
blasphemy which I do not dare to con-
template.'

She did not answer him, and after a
while he proceeded,—

'Don't you think it would be very
wrong of us to marry under the circumstances, Jessie? Don't you think it
may be the wrecking of both our lives
to know there is such a barrier between
us? Don't you think it would be more
honourable in the sight of God and man
for us to go our different ways in the
world, than to take vows upon ourselves
which we know it is not in our power
to perform?'

He paused, waiting for and expecting
her acquiescence; and had the girl
followed the natural instincts of her
womanhood, she would have told him
he was right. But the hint he had

given her of his love for another, vague
and undefined though it was, had raised
the worst feelings of which Jessie
Robertson was capable, and made her
resolve, at all hazards, to claim him for
her own. He should never, *never* (so
she said to herself) be free to go and
marry that other woman, and leave her
to be laughed at or pitied by all their
acquaintance. She loved the man, but
she loved herself better, and she was
determined if possible to keep him by
her side. So all she answered was,—

'*I* could fulfil them, Geoffrey, easily
enough. Nothing could be difficult for
me to do that was done for you.'

'By heavens!' he exclaimed, driven
to desperation by her quiet persever-
ance, 'do you mean to say that you
would stoop to marry me when I tell
you plainly that I do not care for you?'

'Yes, Geoffrey, I would; because you
will care for me some day. I am sure
you will.'

'And with the knowledge that I love some one else?'

'It is not pleasant for me to hear, of course,' said Jessie, 'but you will get over it in time—and you were engaged to me first.'

'Then I am to understand,' rejoined the young man gloomily, 'that you desire me to hold to this engagement, of which I have told you frankly I am weary?'

'Because you fail in your promises to me, is that any reason I should fail also?' she replied. 'I should consider myself bound to you, Geoffrey, whether you deserted me or not.'

'And this is your final decision?' asked her companion, with white lips.

'How could I come to any other? I should only be telling a story if I said I did?'

'Jessie! I told Dr and Mrs Robertson that I would abide by what you said. Think once more; for God's sake, think before you answer me! Remember it is the happiness or misery of our whole lives upon which you are deciding. *Are we to be married to each other, or are we not ?'*

He hung upon her reply as the criminal in the dock hangs upon the decision of the jury, and she gave it with apparently as little personal feeling.

'If you ask *me*, Geoffrey, I can only say what I have said before, *Yes.* If I hadn't wished to marry you, I should never have consented to be engaged to you. I don't change my mind every other day, as you seem to do!'

'God forgive you!' was trembling on his lips as he regarded her, but with an effort he altered the words. 'Be it so, then!' he said, between his teeth; and then, without another look, he turned upon his heel and quitted the house, leaving Jessie Robertson to announce to her father and mother the determination at which she had arrived.

CHAPTER III.

DESERTED.

'Castalio ! Oh, how often has he sworn
Nature should change—the sun and stars grow dark—
E'er he would falsify his vows to me?
Make haste, confusion, then !   Sun, lose thy light !
And stars, drop dead with sorrow to the earth !
For my Castalio's false.'

Otway.

THE long-expected letter from Mentone, addressed to Eliza Bennett, arrived but a few days after Geoffrey Doyne had quitted Ines-cedwyn.   Lady Wilson's party had finished their wanderings for the present, and were settled in the Villa Abracci, but the event did not seem to have fulfilled the expectations of Mrs Barrington, who

complained bitterly of all her surroundings.
The heat was intolerable ; the house had
not sufficient accommodation ; that odious
Miss Russell had joined their party, and
was making herself most conspicuous with
Mr Wilson ; poor dear Colonel Ellerman
had died suddenly of bronchitis the week
before ; and those brutes of agents had
written from London to say that the tenants in South Audley Street wished to
give up the rooms at the end of three
months. In fact, poor Mrs Barrington's
star was decidedly in the descendent.

'Only fancy !' she wrote, 'those wretches
giving up the rooms in July—the very
month of all others when nobody wishes
to remain in London. I made sure they
would renew their agreement until Mich-
aelmas. I think it is most inconsiderate
of them, not to say dishonest—for there
is no chance of my letting the rooms
again. And what are we to do with ourselves in London at that time—you and
I and Fenella ? We shall be roasted alive.

I should remain here, of course, or go on
to some livelier place, only I am afraid
I shall not be able to afford it. I hope to
goodness you and the girl are not running
into any expense that you can possibly
avoid, for all my money has gone in rail-
way fares, and the people here change
their dresses so many times a day, I
haven't half enough clothes to wear. I
consider that Lady Wilson ought, at the
very least, to offer to pay my expenses
back to England, for she has quite brought
me here on false pretences. The weekly
expenses are much higher than she said
they would be, and she has given the best
bedroom in the house to that hideous
Anna Russell—after saying she couldn't
receive Fenella, too. Such deceit! And
the son is exactly like his mother—stingy
and false! I hate them both. I was
dreadfully distressed to hear about your
leg. You really should be more careful.
It is selfish of you to go falling about in
that way, when you know how I depend

upon your services. What would you
have done if I had required you to join
me at Mentone? It's just a chance that
I did not. Lady Wilson's maid is a fool;
she can't dress hair a bit, and the old
woman is so selfish, she will hardly ever
let her do any sewing for me. I often
wish I had Fenella here to help me with
needlework. I hope you or she will write
soon and let me hear that your leg is
healed again. I couldn't stand crutches
about the house. And I'm sure I've had
trouble enough already. You may fancy
the shock dear Colonel Ellerman's death
was to me. So sudden and so sad! And
he's left every halfpenny he possessed to
his sister, too; it makes me so mad to
think of it. However, I suppose it's the
will of Heaven. I am glad to hear your
account of Miss Fenella's looks. It is
just as well one of the family should enjoy
good health. I feel ill and weak enough
myself. I am sure this place doesn't agree
with me, and Lady Wilson is the worst

housekeeper I ever met. The dinners are simply not fit to eat.'

Eliza Bennett was as distressed by the receipt of this letter as if she took every word of it for gospel.

'Your poor dear mamma!' she exclaimed; 'what worries she has in this life, to be sure! And to think that I am not with her, too! that is the cruellest part of it. Not that I could hope to be of much good (being only a servant), but still it's hard for a lady who's been used to have every comfort about her, to wait on herself, and eat dinners she don't fancy; isn't it, Miss Fenella?'

'Mamma might have had us both with her if she had wished it; it's her own fault that she's alone!' replied Fenella, with her eyes fixed upon the summer sky, and her heart filled to the very brim with Geoffrey Doyne.

'Lor'! Miss Fenella, you seem to have grown very cold-like lately,' remarked the servant. 'You fretted so at parting with

your mamma, I thought you'd be all in a
flutter at the idea of meeting her again.
Wouldn't you like to go back to London,
miss ? '

The girl's face flushed with the sudden
joy of expectation. London was the
happy place that held her lover.

' To *London*, nurse ! Oh yes, I should ;
very much indeed. But is there any
chance of it ? '

' Well, I should say from your mamma's
letter as there was every chance, my dear ;
for here we are in the middle of July, and
even if she don't come back herself, some
one must go and look after them rooms
as soon as they're empty.'

' Let me write and tell mamma that we
will look after them,' cried Fenella impul-
sively, ' and then she needn't come home
any sooner on that account. Let us go
back to London together, nurse—you and
I ; it will be ever so much nicer than
Ines-cedwyn.'

Eliza Bennett looked in the girl's tell-tale face, and thought to herself. 'That there chap's in London, I'd take my oath of it ;' but all she said was,—

'You can write what you please to your mamma, Miss Fenella ; but we couldn't go back, at any rate, till the end of July, for the parties don't give up the rooms till that time.'

And her young mistress turned from her with a sigh, to console herself by writing a long letter to Geoffrey Doyne, in which she informed him of her mother's permanent address, and begged him to lose no time in acquainting her with the news of their engagement.

The letters which came and went so constantly at this period, no less than the gold locket which Fenella wore next her heart both night and day, had not escaped the notice of Eliza Bennett, and they made her feel very uneasy. She could not be quite sure of what was going on beneath her eyes—whether it was a mere childish folly, not worth a second

thought, or something more serious, that
would raise Mrs Barrington's anger. The
amourettes of that lady herself had been
so profuse and vicarious, that she had
somewhat dulled thereby the sense of
propriety in the breast of her servant;
and Bennett was really unable to decide whether her mistress would ridicule
her fears or blame her imprudence on
the score of Fenella's sea-side flirtation.
Yet she could not help observing that
the girl had grown more thoughtful since
the young man's departure, and she had
detected her on more than one occasion
crying quietly to herself. She had heard
her talk in her sleep, too—murmuring
broken sentences and loving words, as
she lay flushed on her pillows, with her
fair hair falling on her shoulders, and
the child-like tears still trembling on her
lashes. And yet, withal, Fenella seemed
so happy and so well, it was difficult to
believe that anything grieved her. So
Bennett comforted herself with the idea

that, if her young lady *had* had a little love affair, she'd soon forget all about it. Girls had many such, as a rule, before they settled down in life; and, at any rate, the gentleman had left Ines-cedwyn —that was one blessing—and it couldn't be long now before her mamma came back to England to look after her herself.

Meanwhile, Fenella was what she seemed — as happy as she could be apart from Geoffrey. For these great loves pay heavy penalties for the bliss of being; they render separation an agony. But the tears which Bennett saw upon her sleeping face were not those of distrust, nor of fear. They were the natural outcome of a new-born excitement, that found its best relief in painless weeping. The days of separation were irksome to bear, but they were not intolerable; for Fenella had a firm belief in their speedy termination, and each one brought her some fresh assurance of Geoffrey's love for her.

For here the man's courage had utterly failed him. He knew he had pledged himself to do that which should kill all the new-born blossoming hopes in Fenella's breast, as certainly as a knife drawn across her throat would destroy the fair young life she had given up to him. He knew that in a few weeks at the furthest, she would hear that, that would desecrate him in her eyes for evermore; that would make him appear falser and more cruel than anything she had ever dreamt of; that would destroy, not only her belief in him, but in God and Heaven, and even a hereafter. He knew all this, as surely as he knew that he was committing the basest action of his life in deserting her; and yet he had not the courage to strike the fatal blow, and let her learn the worst at once. He continued to write to her, and without a hint that he had renewed his engagement with Jessie Robertson. He told no further falsehoods, it is true; he ceased to allude to their own marriage, or their future life; but he told her she was his world, and that without her he should be miserable; and Fenella could imagine the rest. To be Geoffrey's world was sufficient for her happiness, and, naturally, she continued to believe that all they had spoken of together would follow. The only shadow on her joy was their prolonged separation, and that was soon to be put an end to.

Mrs Barrington's first letter from Mentone was speedily followed by another, equally querulous, in which she told her daughter and servant that she had had a violent quarrel with Lady Wilson, who was, without exception, ' the most jealous, cross-grained, interfering old cat' she ever met with, and affirmed her intention of returning to England as soon as ever the rooms in South Audley Street were ready to receive her, ordering Bennett and Fenella at the same time to take up their abode there before herself.

'The agent tells me,' she wrote, 'that the creatures will go out on the thirty-first. You had better, therefore, travel up on the first, and I will join you on the second or third. I wouldn't sleep in my room until you have seen it is thoroughly cleaned and set in its usual order, for any earthly consideration.'

To see the colour that flew into Fenella's face at this intelligence was a revelation. She glowed like a carnation at the very thought.

'On the first, Bennett! We are to go to London on the first of August!' she exclaimed; 'only five days more. What shall I do to make them pass away?'

'You seem very anxious to leave poor Ines-cedwyn, miss,' remarked Bennett curiously. 'I'm afraid you've changed your mind about it since you first came here.'

The girl turned her grey eyes, in which the tears had suddenly risen, towards the sea.

'Dear, sweet Ines-cedwyn!' she murmured, 'with its singing waves and golden sands. Can it ever seem less lovely to me than it does now? Oh no, nurse! I have not changed my mind, and I am not ungrateful. I shall always remember Ines-cedwyn as the place in which the happiest days of my life were passed; only—only,' she added, a little wistfully, 'I *do* want to go to London now.'

'Well, my dear, I hope as you won't be disappointed in it, but it's very hot and dusty at this time of the year,' grumbled Bennett, as she turned away.

Yet when the first of August arrived, and Fenella found herself once more in South Audley Street, with all the rooms in that delightful state of dirt and confusion in which lodgers are accustomed to leave them, and Bennett out of temper at the prospect of the work before her, she still went singing about to that unheard accompaniment of music in her heart.

Geoffrey was not there to meet her, it is true (how could he be?), but he was close at hand, and she had received a letter from him, not twelve hours before she left Ines-cedwyn, full of love and tender allusions to the past. And she had written in reply to say that she was there, actually *there*, in the same town with him; and it could not be long—it was impossible it could be long—before he held her in his arms. Mrs Barrington arrived to her time — dusty, dishevelled, and decidedly cross. But she could not restrain her surprise at the first view of Fenella.

'Good heavens!' she exclaimed, 'what have you done to the child, Bennett? Why, she's developed to a woman; and what a lovely colour she has! I must say it, my dear; your complexion would put the whole of Piver's shop to shame. It is positively like nothing but lilies and carnations.'

'Oh, mamma! I am so glad you think

I am improved,' said Fenella, with a bright blush, as she knelt beside Mrs Barrington's chair. 'I have been so happy down at Ines-cedwyn; I think that must be the reason that I look so well.'

'It's the mountain air and the smell of the sea, ma'am,' put in Eliza Bennett, rather hurriedly; 'it *must* be, for I am sure Miss Fenella has had no other doctors whilst you was away.'

'Well, I wish I had had the same doctors myself, for I'm worn to death with my trip,' replied her mistress fretfully. 'Do get up, Fenella; you're dragging my dress to one side, and I'm too tired to bear the weight of your arms upon my knees. I'm sure I wish I had never left London. I've lost all the fun of the season, and now I suppose we shall have to vegetate here whilst everybody is away at the sea-side.'

'We shall manage to amuse ourselves, mamma, surely,' said Fenella, smiling, as she thought of the occupation which was

in store for both of them, in preparing
for her wedding with Geoffrey Doyne.

'You don't know what you're talking
about, child. Everybody is out of town
at this time of the year, and the place is
so hot and dusty, you can hardly stir out
of the house. However, we must bear
it as best we can, for there's no alterna-
tive. I can't go through the trouble and
worry of letting the rooms again, and if I
did so, I don't know where on earth we
should go.'

'Oh no, mamma! don't think of it,'
cried Fenella. 'We shall be very happy
here—I am sure we shall—and there's
no knowing what may turn up to amuse
and occupy us.'

But when Mrs Barrington found herself
alone with her favourite servant, she told
a very different story.

'Bennett,' she said confidentially, 'I
didn't like to say too much before the
girl (for girls are always so conceited
about their personal appearance), but I

never was so startled in my life as when I saw Fenella. I couldn't have believed three months would make such a change in any one. She's positively *lovely;* I have seen nothing to equal her in Paris or Mentone! And so fresh too; it's what the men run after now-a-days, freshness! I shall let these rooms again as soon as ever I can, Bennett, and take her abroad.'

'Let the rooms again, ma'am!' echoed Bennett. 'I thought as you said you had decided against it?'

'So I did at first, you old goose; but don't you see I shall have a better chance of marrying that girl now than at any other period of her existence. Three months ago no man would have looked at her—she was a child, a stick, a nonentity! But now they would just rave about her. She has unfolded like a rosebud opened this morning. She's in the first flush of girlhood, and yet she's a woman! You can see it by her eyes. I never was

so astonished in the world before! What's
done it, Bennett? Has she had a love
affair at Ines-cedwyn?'

'Oh, dear no, ma'am!' gasped Bennett,
trembling from head to foot under the
dread of discovery.

'Ah well, I suppose it's nature; but
I must say she's lovely, though I'm her
mother. Whom does she take most
after, Bennett—me, or the poor captain?
I was always the fairer of the two, you
know.'

'Oh yes, ma'am; and Miss Fenella
favours you wonderfully, especially about
the skin. I don't know as I ever saw
such another skin as hers; it's like
white satin.'

'And her figure's very fine too; and
men think so much of figures now-a-days.
Everybody can have a pretty face who
knows how to "make up" properly; but
you can't have a good figure in an evening dress, unless Heaven has given it to
you. It would be an *immense* thing for

me if I could marry Miss Fenella well,
and without delay, Bennett—an *immense*
thing. It would just save me from ruin,
and nothing else. And she *ought* to go
off! Dressed in white and silver, or
white and gold, she would look splendid!
glorious! I believe I could turn out
that girl so that no one could come
within a mile of her; and it would be
worth my while to do it, at any price!
How can we manage it, Bennett? Do
ransack that good old head of yours, and
find out some means by which we can
carry on the war for a few months longer,
until I have introduced her at Trouville
or Baden, or some of those places where
the best men go. And she speaks French
so perfectly, that she might marry a
foreigner and a title—one of those rich
nobles who frequent the watering-places
through the autumn months—and I should
get her off my hands and out of my way
at the same time.'

'Yes, yes! my dear lady. We will

manage it. Never you fear,' replied the
servant, in a soothing tone.

She generally treated her mistress as
if she were a teething child that required conciliation ; but the only childish
thing about Mrs Barrington was her
refractoriness. In all other things Eliza
Bennett was as spun silk in her hands.

'You're so tired with your journey,
ma'am,' she continued. 'You mustn't
think of anything now but getting rested.
And you've had nothing to eat to-day,
so to speak, and yet you turned against
your dinner ! Shall I run out and get
you a little lobster with a dash of salad,
and a glass of champagne, and see if
that will tempt you to pick a bit ? '

'Yes, if you like, Bennett,' returned
the lady languidly, 'for I really don't
feel as if I could keep on my legs much
longer.'

'Lie down, my dear mistress,' exclaimed the servant anxiously, 'and
don't move till I've brought you some-

thing to eat. There! let me loose your
hair, and give you a fan and the eau
de Cologne. And would you like Miss
Fenella to sit with you, ma'am, whilst
I'm away?'

'No, Bennett, thank you. I shall do
very well. I feel as if I were at home
again, now I have you to cosset me and
look after me. I'm a poor creature, and
cannot live without love.'

The servant's plain face glowed with
ardour.

'You will always have *mine*, my
dear, *dear* lady,' she replied.

'Ah well, I hope I may, Bennett; but the world is very ungrateful, and the best friends change sometimes. You would be surprised to see
the alteration in those horrid Wilsons.
The old woman hardly spoke to me
the last week I was in Mentone; and
as for her son, his behaviour was positively disgusting. He and that odious
creature Anna Russell used to leave

the house directly after breakfast, and
never reappear till dinner-time. It was
most improper, as I told his mother, and
then we had a fight about it. I can't
stand that sort of people, Bennett;
they're low-bred and presuming, and
directly they find a cause for quarrel,
their bad blood comes to the front. I
shall never call upon Lady Wilson again.'

'No, my dear lady; I hope you won't.
You've been too good and condescend-
ingly to her already. And you mustn't
think no more of Mr Wilson either.
He ain't worthy of the likes of you!'

'Dear me, no! Of course that's all
over. And poor Colonel Ellerman too.
It's enough to upset a woman (isn't it,
Bennett?) losing two of them so near
together, and so unexpectedly!'

'Ah! there's as good fish in the sea
as ever came out of it, ma'am; and,
please the Lord! I shall live to see
you riding over the heads of such people
as the Wilsons yet.'

'Well, if I can only get Miss Fenella married and out of the way, I think I shall have as good a chance as any. By-the-bye, Bennett, as you go for the lobster, you might as well look in at the agents, and tell them to put the rooms on their books again. Say I'll let them on any reasonable terms, for I know I can't get a high rent at this time of the year. But I'm determined to take that girl abroad, Bennett, if I pawn my jewellery to accomplish it. After all, it would be worth my while, for I could get it out again as soon as ever she was married.'

Filled with this new idea, Mrs Barrington became so friendly and confidential with her daughter, that Fenella (remembering her first reception) was agreeably surprised. She did not know the little plot that was hatching beneath her mother's flattering notice of her beauty or her talents. She believed it to be genuine. And so, in part, it was. Mrs Barrington could not live without some excitement, and Fenella's improved appearance had suggested a new excitement to her. Having a handsome *demoiselle à marier* to take about and add a fresh attraction to her own society, was a different thing altogether from being annoyed by the presence of a half-formed school-girl, whom no man would wish to own either by marriage or adoption. And the notion having once entered her head, she became crazy to put it into execution.

Fenella was pleased and startled, at first, by her mother's cordiality towards her; but as the days went on without bringing tidings of Geoffrey Doyne, her spirits began to sink. She had not the slightest doubt of her lover, but her heart was filled with every sort of fear for him. Was it possible, she thought, that he had never received her last letter from Inescedwyn? Was he still sending his to the old address? and was Martha too stupid to forward them to London? Could he

be ill, or dying ?—(the ignorant imagine no
greater calamity than death can befall
those whom they love)—or had his family
refused their consent to his marriage, and
was he afraid to come and break the news
to her ?   These, and a hundred other
doubts that made her heart sick with
apprehension, surged and swayed through
Fenella's bosom, until she felt as if she
must seek Geoffrey out at all hazards,
and learn the truth.   But that the truth
could involve anything worse than annoyance, or delay, never entered her mind.
How could it—with Geoffrey ?

Her mother and she kept very close
to the house during those few days of
suspense.   Mrs Barrington (who was
naturally lazy and untidy) never appeared
en grande tenue unless there was something to be gained by it, and considered
a soiled dressing-gown the proper costume
to wear during a month when nobody was
likely to call, and there was no object in
showing herself abroad.   She sat indoors,

therefore, all day fanning herself, and making calculations for her proposed autumn manœuvres; whilst Fenella read novels from the circulating library, or the contents of the newspapers, aloud to her.

One evening during the first week they spent in London, the girl was sitting with a very heavy heart, trying thus to amuse her mother. She had stolen out that afternoon, and slipped a letter in the post herself — imploring Geoffrey to let her know at once whether he had received the news of her arrival in town. And now she felt almost numbed by the suspense of waiting for an answer, as if life or death hung on the chance of her receiving it by return of post.

'I think that story's abominably stupid,' said Mrs Barrington presently. 'The man's a stick, and the woman's a goody. Don't you think so, Fenella?'

'Eh! what, mamma? Oh yes, I do!' exclaimed Fenella suddenly, as she caught the meaning of her mother's words.

' I don't think you're enjoying it much
more than I am, my dear, and I don't
wonder at it,' resumed Mrs Barrington.
' The last chapter has been a perfect ser-
mon, and I hate preaching, especially in a
novel.   Suppose you read me the paper instead ? I haven't had time to look at it to-
day. You'll find the *Standard* on that table.'

Fenella put down the novel and rose to
fetch the paper, with that heart-sickening
suspense (which those who have expe-
rienced the feeling will best recognise)
still uppermost in her mind.

' Let's have the epitome of news,' said
Mrs Barrington, as the girl reseated herself.   ' Or stay, Fenella ; read the list of
marriages and deaths first.   Not the
births, my dear (nobody cares about
births except the people concerned ; they're
much too common) ; but you see lots of
names amongst the marriages and deaths
of people you have heard of, though you
may not know.   Just run over the names
as they stand, Fenella ; that will be quite

enough. Dear me! I wish my sight were not so weak by gas light. It makes me feel quite an old woman to be so dependent on others.'

The girl began to read as she was ordered :—Adams—Messiter ; Arbuthnott — Clive ; Barclay — Smith ; Cadogan — Matthews ; Doyne — Robertson. And there she stopped.

'Go on, my dear,' said her mother somewhat impatiently.

But Fenella did not go on. Her eyes were staring in a blank vacuous manner at the following words :—

'August 3rd, at the Church of St Mary le Strand, by the Rev. ——, Geoffrey Doyne, Lieut. H.M. XXX. Regiment of Hussars, second son of Jasper Doyne, J.P., of Ryelands, in the county of Buckinghamshire ; to Jessie, fourth daughter of James Robertson, M.D., of 44 Blenheim Square, W.C.'

Mrs Barrington could not stand the suspense.

'Do go on, Fenella,' she repeated irritably; 'it drives me wild when people stop in the middle of reading in that way. Whatever have you got there—anything interesting?'

But all the answer she received was conveyed by the sound of a heavy fall. Fenella had fainted on the floor. At this sight Mrs Barrington became terribly alarmed. She was a woman who lost all presence of mind in an emergency.

'Bennett! Bennett!' she screamed, flying to the door, 'come down here at once. Miss Fenella has fainted.'

The servant was in the room in a minute, and kneeling beside the unconscious girl.

'Why, bless my heart alive!' she exclaimed, 'how did this happen?'

'I don't know, I'm sure,' wailed Mrs Barrington; 'she was reading the *Standard* to me only a minute ago, when she suddenly fell on the floor. Oh dear! oh dear! I hope she's not going to take to fainting; it's the most tiresome habit a girl can have; you never know when it'll come on. Did you see anything of this in the country, Bennett?'

'Bless you, no, ma'am! And don't go to frighten yourself; it's only an accident. Young ladies will faint sometimes. It's the heat of the weather most likely, or Miss Fenella has over-tired herself. We must lay her down flat, that's the best way; and please to give me the eau de Cologne and your fan, and I'll soon bring her to.'

But though Eliza Bennett made every effort to restore Fenella to consciousness, twenty minutes elapsed, and still the girl lay, rigid as stone and white as a broken lily, prostrate upon the ground.

'I don't like this, ma'am,' said Bennett, shaking her head as she found her restoratives had no effect. 'I am afraid it is more than an ordinary swoon. Don't you think we'd better send round for Dr Metcalfe?'

'It *surely* can't be necessary,' replied her mistress. 'Oh! don't tell me there's more trouble in store for us, Bennett, and I'm to have a doctor's bill added to my other worries. Dash some more water in her face. I'm sure she blinked last time you did it. Perhaps she's only shamming. Girls *will* sham sickness, you know, sometimes. They think it's interesting!'

'Miss Fenella ain't shamming,' said the servant indignantly; 'and indeed, ma'am, you *must* please to send Mrs Watson for the doctor, for I can't take the responsibility of this on myself any longer.

Mrs Barrington was frightened into concession, and the medical man, who lived close at hand, was soon in the room. He raised Fenella's head and looked in her face.

'Cut her dress and her laces,' he said curtly.

'Oh dear, sir, they're as loose as they can be!' remonstrated Bennett.

'Be good enough to do as I tell you,' was the reply; and when she had obeyed him, he lifted the girl upon the couch, and laid his ear upon her chest.

'That will do,' he said presently, as he rose to his feet; 'and now, where is her bedroom? I will carry her up to bed.'

Bennett led the way, and Dr Metcalfe lifted the girl's slight figure in his arms, and followed her. The mother was left behind, wringing her hands in feeble lamentation.

'I hope to goodness this is not the beginning of an illness,' she thought self- ishly, 'for it will ruin all my plans if Fenella goes and loses her good looks just as she requires them most.'

Presently she heard Dr Metcalfe's foot- step descending the stairs again, and waited near the door in expectation of his entering to give her further informa- tion about her daughter. But he passed her landing and walked straight out of the house.

'Such extraordinary behaviour,' as Mrs Barrington said to her servant a few minutes later ; 'just as if I had no concern in the matter, and wasn't even the girl's mother! But what did he say upstairs, Bennett? Is this fainting fit a mere accident, or is it likely to occur again? I shall go mad if she takes to having them as a regular thing.'

'Oh no, ma'am! it won't be as bad as that ; but I'm bound to say the doctor looked grave about it, and he'll see Miss Fenella the first thing to-morrow morning. It was terrible to watch her come-to, ma'am. I thought she was going out of her mind. But the doctor give her a powerful sleeping draught, and she dropped off like a child. But I don't think he likes the looks of her at all.'

'It is *I* that shall go out of my mind with all this worry,' cried Mrs Barrington. 'However, I don't believe she *can* be really ill with that lovely colour, and I daresay Dr Metcalfe is making all the fuss he can over it, just to run up a bill. It's the way with those doctors — once get into their hands, and you never get out again.'

'I am afraid I must go back to Miss Fenella now, ma'am,' said Bennett; 'for the doctor's orders are that she's not to be left for a minute, and she's to stay in bed till after he's seen her to-morrow.'

'Of course,' replied Mrs Barrington petulantly. 'I knew how it would be. I'm to lose *you* now, and wait on myself, I suppose. Oh! these children! these children! what a plague and a nuisance they are, to be sure!'

But the affectionate mother enjoyed a good night's rest, notwithstanding her anxiety, although her servant sat beside her daughter's bed until the morning. The report she then made to her mistress was anything but reassuring.

'I can't make Miss Fenella out at all, ma'am,' she said; 'she opened her eyes a good while since, but she's never turned in her bed, nor spoken a word to me. She looks *fixed* like, and I do hope the

doctor will keep his promise to come and
see her.'

The doctor did keep his promise, and
at ten o'clock Bennett tapped again on
her mistress's door.

'Dr Metcalfe is here, if you please,
ma'am, and he's seen Miss Fenella, and
he'd like to speak a few words with you
before he leaves the house.'

'Very well, Bennett ; just tie a ribbon
in my hair, and give me that blue shawl.
You must tell the doctor I'm *en deshabille*,
you know ; but I've been too terribly
anxious about the dear child to think of
my dress.'

Mrs Barrington repeated something to
the same effect when the doctor entered
her room, but was unable to extract a
compliment from him in return. He took
all her excuses literally.

'You have every cause for anxiety,
madam,' he answered gravely, 'and I am
afraid that what I have to tell you will
increase instead of diminish it. I am

sorry to say that I find Miss Barrington
in a very unsatisfactory state of health.
I believe she has spent this summer away
from you?'

'Yes; I sent her to Ines-cedwyn, a
most charming place in Wales, under the
charge of my own maid, who was formerly
her nurse. I thought the dear girl required sea air, and so I forced myself to
make the sacrifice of parting with her.
But it is one of the healthiest spots in
the world. Surely she cannot have con-
tracted any illness there?'

'Miss Barrington's present attack,
madam, is more mental than physical,' replied Dr Metcalfe, 'but I can tell you the
cause from which it has sprung. You must
not think I am meddling with your private
affairs in speaking plainly, but I consider
it my duty to let you know the truth.'

He posed himself opposite to her, with
one arm leaning on the mantelpiece, whilst
he entered into a detail of Fenella's symp-
toms.

Mrs Barrington listened to him in silence—an angry and indignant silence—feeling with each word he uttered that the fabric of her hopes crumbled into smaller atoms. Fenella with *une affaire de cœur;* the girl for whom she had formed such ambitious projects, breaking her heart for some nameless nobody in the wilds of Wales; *her* daughter, struck to the ground by some stupid flirtation that had made itself patent to the eyes of the first stranger she had called in to prescribe a soothing draught. It was too disappointing, too humiliating. At the idea of it Mrs Barrington went pale beneath her rage, and trembled from head to foot.

'I am afraid I have wounded you,' said Dr Metcalfe kindly, as he concluded, 'but it was impossible to help doing so. As her mother, I considered it only right that I should speak openly to you.'

'Oh yes! of course—of course,' stammered Mrs Barrington; and then she added, ' I was just thinking of taking her abroad.'

The doctor caught at the idea.

' The very best thing you could do for her, Mrs Barrington. You must be aware that in these cases change of air and scene, and a little seclusion—unless, indeed, any attachment the young lady may have formed might be brought to a happy issue instead. But I am sure I need not hint at such alternatives to you. Your own heart and your affection for your daughter will prove better guides in such a contingency than any advice you could receive from strangers.'

But all Mrs Barrington said was,—

' I conclude there will be no further need of your attendance, Dr Metcalfe, and we shall leave town as soon as possible.'

' Certainly, madam ! I had no intention of calling again. May I express a hope of seeing you and Miss Barrington at some future time, and under pleasanter circumstances ? '

He gave her his hand as he spoke, and she thrust a fee into it.

'But it will be the last,' she thought angrily, as he disappeared; 'never shall he cross my threshold again after what he has said to me to-day.'

She sat for some time where the doctor had left her—too paralysed, apparently, to move or speak. The first thing that roused her from her reverie was the sound of the opening door. As it turned on its hinges. Eliza Bennett's face peeped wistfully into the room.

'Is the doctor gone, ma'am?' she demanded.

The question seemed to goad Mrs Barrington into action. She sprang to her feet, and confronted the terrified servant with the face of a fury.

'Is the doctor gone?' she repeated. 'Yes, he *is* gone; and do you know what he came to tell me? That you have been faithless to the trust I reposed in you, and that whilst I thought that

wretched girl upstairs was safe under
your care, you let her go rushing all
over the place by herself just as she
chose, and making love to every cockney
tourist that came in her way.'

'*I*, ma'am—*I?*' gasped Eliza Bennett,
panic-stricken by the accusation. 'Oh,
don't go to say that of *me*, ma'am, when
you know I was laid up in my bed, unable to lift hand or foot for five weeks
at a stretch, and knew no more of what
was going on outside than the babe un-
born.'

'Then you *ought* to have known,'
thundered her mistress, 'or set some one
else to look after her! You've behaved
most treacherously to me, and all the
harm that comes of this will be laid at
your door.'

'But what has Miss Fenella done,
ma'am? I'm sure if a young lady like
her is not to be trusted on a beach
alone, who is?'

'What has she done? It is you who

should be able to answer that question. Whom did she meet? Who did she see down there? What man has dared to make love to her? That is what I want to know.'

Bennett's thoughts flew at once to the gentleman in the Beach Bungalow—the letters and the locket; but she considered it her duty to Fenella to stand firm to her ground.

'Nobody, ma'am,' she answered; 'that *I'm* sure of! How *should* there be, when Ines-cedwyn's such a lonely place? We were the only visitors there this summer.'

'You'd better first hear what Dr Metcalfe has told me,' replied her mistress; and she repeated the statement of the medical man for the benefit of the servant.

Bennett's face became as white as chalk during the narration.

'Will you still insist in maintaining that you know nothing of the matter?' demanded Mrs Barrington angrily.

'I don't believe it's true—and I know nothing about it,' repeated the servant stoutly.

'I'll see if the girl is as obstinate as you are,' exclaimed her mistress, darting upstairs.

Bennett, fearing the scene that might ensue between the mother and daughter, followed her quickly, and reached the spot as soon as she did.

Fenella was standing in the centre of the room, supporting herself with one hand against the iron railing at the foot of the bed. The dressing-gown she wore was not whiter than her complexion; her hair was tossed in the wildest confusion over her breast and shoulders; her grey eyes had a scared and piteous look in them, as if she had just awakened from some hideous dream. It was evident that she had guessed, or overheard, the substance of the communication which Dr Metcalfe had made to her mother.

Mrs Barrington advanced upon the

trembling girl with the air of a virago.

'Well!' she exclaimed, in a shrill, coarse voice (it is astonishing how coarse the most delicate and apparently well-bred women can be when their tempers are raised), 'are you not ashamed to stand there staring at me in that brazen way, when the whole town is ringing with your disgrace? Do you know what the doctor has told me? Oh, don't pretend to shrink, and be extra modest, after the bold manner in which you have been conducting yourself. You're a nice young lady to be trusted to go about alone, flirting with every low fisherman you may meet upon the beach! Tell me the name of the man who dared to make love to you at Ines-cedwyn, you innocent piece of goods! you—'

But Fenella did not speak. She continued still and rigid as a figure of marble, with her eyes fixed upon vacancy.

'Do you hear what I say to you?' screamed Mrs Barrington. 'Tell me the

name of the man who presumed to make
love to my daughter (though he never
would have done so if you hadn't given
him encouragement), and I will have him
whipped through the streets like a hound.
Henry Wilson would do it for me, if he were
not a cur himself—or Colonel Ellerman,
only he's dead. Good heavens! what did
your father mean by dying in that stupid
manner, and leaving us to look after such
things for ourselves? Why haven't we a
man to fight our battles for us? But you
shall tell me the name of that fellow, or I'll
shake it out of you.'

Still the girl's mouth did not unclose,
and Bennett, who was watching her anxiously, saw her white teeth press upon her
under lip until she made the blood come.
It was evident that she was resolved to
keep her own secret.

'Oh! you're obstinate, are you?' exclaimed Mrs Barrington, 'and you will try
to defy me! You think you can bring all
this trouble upon our heads with impunity;

that you can go tumbling about the house
and fainting, and being threatened with a
brain attack, for the sake of some 'disgraceful love affair that you ought to be
ashamed to think of; and I'm to pass it
over, and take you to my arms again,
and say you're a very good girl! I'll tell
you *what* I say, and that is that you're a
born idiot! Just as I was going to take
you to Paris or Brussels, too, and introduce
you to society! And now, you may be ill
for months, you ungrateful, wicked girl!
But I am not going to be fooled by
you! You shall tell the name of that
man, if you die for it.'

She advanced threateningly upon the
passive figure of Fenella as she spoke,
and Bennett laid her hand upon her
arm.

'She's really ill, ma'am,' she whispered.
'Pray be careful what you do to her; you
may bring on another attack.'

But her mistress was in no mood to
accept advice. She shook off Eliza

Bennett's touch as if it had been that of à scorpion.

'Leave me alone! How dare you interfere?' she said angrily. 'I shall deal with my own daughter as I choose;' and then she turned again upon the girl. 'Do as I order you!' she exclaimed. 'Tell me the name of your lover at once, or I'll strike you!' and, lifting her arm, she brought it down with her utmost force against the white, sad face that confronted her.

Fenella did not utter a word of entreaty or remonstrance. She only shivered violently as the blow descended, and, sitting down upon the nearest chair, passed her own hand in a sort of wondering way across her eyes and forehead.

'Oh, Lor', ma'am! you do frighten me!' said Bennett. 'Let her be, my dear lady, at least for the present. She ain't in a fit state to listen to you; indeed, she ain't!'

'It's evident whose side *you're* on,' replied her mistress witheringly ; 'but you'll do the girl no good by your partisanship, and that I can tell you. She has behaved in a manner to disgrace us all ; and if she were dead and cold in her coffin, it would be the best thing that could happen to her.'

Then, for the first time, Fenella found her voice.

'Oh, mother! mother!' she wailed, 'pity me.'

But she might as well have appealed to a stone.

'*Pity you!*' repeated Mrs Barrington, with a sneer. '*Despise* you, you mean. You won't find many to pity you for having ruined all your prospects in life. They will only laugh at and ridicule you for being such a fool. But if this lover of yours is a gentleman, and can be called to account for his treachery to you, he shall. If you want me to pity you, you must tell me his name; and, as your mother, I command you to do so.'

But Fenella had again relapsed into silence. Eliza Bennett tried the effect of coaxing.

'Come, my dear,' she said; 'I daresay it'll be hard-like, but you'd better confide everything to your mamma. She's your best friend, Miss Fenella, and it's useless trying to keep the truth back from her.'

The girl shook her head.

'It wouldn't be any good,' she said simply.

'Nonsense!' replied Mrs Barrington. 'A child like you is no judge of such matters, and, as Bennett tells you, I am your best friend. Come, Fenella, tell me this man's name, and if things can be set right between you, they shall. I am sorry I slapped you, but you really are too provoking. However, I'll look over everything that has passed between us, if you will place confidence in me now.'

And Mrs Barrington, who was intensely curious in the matter, lowered her head so that her daughter might whisper in her ear.

'It would be useless,' repeated Fenella, in a low voice of pain.

'Why useless? Your obstinacy surpasses anything I have ever seen for a girl of your age. I tell you it is *not* useless. What makes you persist that it is so?'

'Because — because *he is married*,' said Fenella, with an effort that seemed to drag at her very heart-strings.

'*Married!*' screamed Mrs Barrington. 'The disgraceful, dishonourable creature! And *you*, you shameless girl! what did you mean by letting a married man make love to you? I never heard of such abominable iniquity in all my life before. Here! have I lived to the age of thirty years, or a little over, and

travelled about the world, and seen all
sorts of people, and it is left for my
own daughter, a child of sixteen, to
initiate me into the horrors of vice!
Bennett, get me a glass of wine! get
me brandy! get me anything that may
help me to drown this terrible remembrance! Or, stay! Let me leave the
room. I cannot breathe this atmo-
sphere any longer! *A married man!*
That I should have lived to hear such
a thing! I, who have had but one
aim throughout my sorrowful life—to
keep myself and my child unspotted
from the world. May Heaven forgive
you, Fenella!'

And with this solemn adjuration, Mrs
Barrington swept out of the room.

As soon as she had quite disappeared,
Eliza Bennett advanced to the side of
her young mistress. Fenella was seated
where her mother had left her—still,
white, and silent, with her piteous grey
eyes staring at the opposite wall. The

servant laid her rough hand on the girl's soft fingers.

'Pray to God, Miss Fenella,' she said gently. 'He loves you, my dear; He will hear you. Pray to Him, and maybe prayer will bring you comfort.'

Fenella lifted her eyes to those of the old woman wearily.

'*Is* there a God, nurse?' she asked. '*I doubt it.* The reverend mother in the convent used to tell me to pray to the good God, and He would protect me from all harm; and I have prayed to Him regularly, morning and evening, since. But I think He must have stayed behind in the convent, nurse. I don't think He came out into the world— with me.'

CHAPTER IV.

OVER.

'She had fallen in her own sight—not because he
had loved her, but because he had left her.'

Ariadne.

IN the heart of the Wallon there
lies a little village called
Sainte Pauvrette, which is a
mass of flowers and sweet-smelling herbs
in summer, and a mass of snow and ice
in winter. It possesses no baths, no
mineral springs, no objects of historical
interest — nothing, in fact, wherewith to
tempt a visitor except its climate and its
flowers. Tourists who know something
of the country, and wish to get out of

the beaten track of overdone cathedrals
and exhausted picture - galleries, go to
Sainte Pauvrette in the warm weather,
when the hillside is covered with lemon-
scented thyme and feathery sorrel and
ruddy clover, and the surrounding country is redolent of lilies and roses and
honeysuckle ; but no one ever dreams of
remaining there throughout the winter.
When the snow falls, Sainte Pauvrette is
left to the few peasants who till its fields
and pray in its dirty little chapel. The
wooden building that calls itself a hotel
is boarded up and left to take care of
itself ; and the residents who have rooms
to let, lock the doors and retreat to the
lower regions, burrowing like moles until
the sunshine shall tempt them to the
upper world again.

But one day not two months after the
events recorded in the last chapter, the inhabitants of Sainte Pauvrette were astonished by the arrival of two English ladies,
who, with their maid, took up their quarters

in one of the small furnished houses that had just been vacated by the summer visitors, and appeared disposed to settle themselves down there for the winter. The season of Sainte Pauvrette was over.; the autumn, with its usual risk of fever and malaria, was close at hand ; the rooms for hire had been cleaned and shut up for the next six months — and the people of Sainte Pauvrette would as soon have expected their patron saint to appear among them, and demand lodgings for the winter, as to see any more visitors. The circumstance was so unusual and startling that it caused endless talk amongst the villagers, and Madame Regnier (who was the lucky person to let her house to the new-comers) began to think she must be under the especial care of Providence, and that a miracle had been performed in her behalf. But the strangers—Mrs Barrington, Fenella, and Eliza Bennett — kept entirely to themselves, and did not appear disposed

to satisfy the curiosity of their neighbours. The tradespeople, who were
chiefly small farmers, selling their own
milk, bread, vegetables, and poultry, tried
their best to extract some information
from Eliza Bennett, but she was invul-
nerable. Either she could not or she
would not understand what they said to
her, and never did more than haggle
with them over the prices of their mer-
chandise, and carry off her bargains in
her market basket. But the ladies were
often seen about the village, and many
were the conjectures made as to the reason
of their sojourn there.

The young lady was sick. Sainte
Pauvrette decided that point very
speedily. And it was supposed that her
mother had brought her to the village
for the sake of her health. The peasants
soon grew to recognise and smile at the
sweet, sad face of Fenella as she passed
amongst them, and to talk of the girl
who sat sometimes motionless for hours

on the hillside, looking at the horizon with a weary, impassive expression that made their hearts ache.

There were rumours, too, that the mother and daughter did not get on very well together, and Madame Jeanne, the proprietress of the wooden hotel (whose offers of accommodation Mrs Barrington had peremptorily refused), had a good deal to say to her neighbours on the subject of that lady's treatment of Fenella.

' *Ma foi!* ' she would exclaim, as she lounged against the outside wall of her house, knitting stockings of coarse yarn, and surrounded by a bevy of women, all knitting as if their lives depended on it,— ' *ma foi!* but I wouldn't be the daughter of that Englishwoman for a great deal. She has a tongue the length of a cow's tail ; you may hear it from one end of Sainte Pauvrette to the other. And it's my belief that when she gets into a rage, she beats her ! '

'You don't mean to say that!' cried
her neighbours, as they drew closer.

Madame Jeanne nodded her head ora-
cularly.

'But I do! The screams that came
from that house the other night were
fearful. You might have thought there
was murder being committed there, and
so I told the English servant—bah! what
an ogre she is! with never a smile nor
a pleasant look on her face—and she said
her young lady was subject to hysteria.
But I don't believe that. The mother
beats her! take my word for it.'

'The young lady certainly looks very
sad,' interposed another woman. 'She
has the face of an angel, and the air of a
martyr. I was watching her yesterday morning. She sat for two hours on the bench by
the ruined chapel without moving. And in
this cold weather too! It is not natural that
a young girl should neither jump nor run.
But I do not think she could be merry if
she tried. She has a face full of care and

sorrow. And she cannot be more than seventeen or eighteen years old.'

'It is *Madame sa Mère* that gives her that face,' rejoined Madame Jeanne. 'She is a fury, a virago, a devil, that woman, and capable of anything that is bad.'

'She pays the rent regularly, and they are quiet and respectable tenants,' said Madame Regnier, who was naturally on Mrs Barrington's side, 'and you only spread these tales about them, Madame Jeanne, because they would not take rooms in your wooden hotel. And they were quite right too! It is draughty enough in winter to kill a delicate *demoiselle* like Miss Barrington. But you have no right to speak against them on that account; and if you say more, I will inform Père Antoine of your behaviour, and have you openly rebuked for scandal.'

'Bah, pig!' cried Madame Jeanne, opening her black eyes at Madame Regnier, with a *moue* of disdain; 'go to—! Tell the priest and whom you will; but all

your talking will not alter matters. Everybody in Sainte Pauvrette has heard the
quarrels that go on in that house! It was
only the other day that mademoiselle ran
out of it bareheaded, with a great angry
red mark across her face, and would
have traversed the village so, had not
the ogre servant appeared and pulled her
indoors again. They ill-treat *la petite*,
I tell you! She is sick and ailing, poor
child—consumptive, most likely, like all
those English; and they make her miserable. I have seen the tears pouring
down her face like rain. It is a pity she
has no father to defend her! A man is
bad enough when he takes a spite against
you, and knocks you about; but, *ma foi!*
he is nothing to a woman. A bad woman
is a devil, and nothing less, and your
Madame Barrington is a bad woman,
and I say it!—eh, Madame Regnier?
You had better go at once and tell Père
Antoine so, and I'll repeat it to his face.
What d'ye make of that?'

'She pays her rent regularly,' grumbled Madame Regnier, 'so it's not my place to speak against her. And as for the rest, Madame Jeanne, we must each think what we choose about it.'

Whatever they chose to think could hardly have been worse than the reality. The autumn and winter months which she passed in Sainte Pauvrette were such a tumultuous mixture of anger, strife, reproaches, and hopeless misery, that Fenella Barrington, through all the rest of her weary life, could never look back upon them without a shudder—as a man who has passed days and nights of suspense tossing about the cruel ocean, living in the very shadow of death, and beaten upon by all the storms of heaven, might look back and wonder he still lived to tell the tale.

Her mother's conduct to her at this period was the very refinement of cruelty. Had she only struck the wretched girl—as she too often did to satisfy her own

feelings of rage and disappointment—it
would have been as nothing compared
to the sneers and reproaches and abuse
cast at the absent, which were so much
harder to bear. And Fenella could not
say a word in defence of herself or him.
She was condemned to sit and hear it all
in silence, whilst she pressed her hands
upon her aching bosom where the image
of Geoffrey Doyne (though shattered into
fragments) was still cherished as the holiest
thing she had ever possessed.

How often, whilst the villagers of Sainte
Pauvrette watched her sitting on the hillside, motionless for hours, she was longing
to die—praying, in a sort of half-conscious
way, that God would send down His
Angel of Death to take her out of a
world which had opened upon a scene of
so much perplexity and trouble for her.

But Fenella hardly knew what she
really wished for. The present and the
future were alike blanks. All she knew
for certain was that Geoffrey Doyne had

passed out of her life—that he belonged
to another woman—that she should never
see him again, nor hear his voice; and
the mere fact of this knowledge was too
wonderful a mystery for her to fathom.
For she did not even know how it had
happened, or why. Not a line, not a
sound, had reached her since she had read
the public announcement of his marriage;
and sometimes she would wonder, in a
vague, childish way, if it had been all
a dream, and pinch her arm, with a sad
smile, to see if she were real. But then
remembrance would rush back upon her—
rush back with a feeling of shame and
horror that would flood her pale cheeks
with crimson, and retreat as suddenly,
leaving them white with despair.

Eliza Bennett felt deeply for her young
mistress during her illness. Though the
people of Sainte Pauvrette found her
curt and harsh of speech, she only assumed that manner to cover her emotion.
She could hardly trust herself to think

of Fenella, far less to speak of her. Had
she been left to her own devices, she
would have been the tenderest of nurses
and comforters to the forlorn and unhappy girl, but Mrs Barrington would
not permit it. She had her own reasons
for keeping up a sense of her ingratitude
and folly in Fenella's breast. She wanted
to force her daughter to throw off the
disappointment and depression under
which she laboured, and make her thankful to rush back into the world as soon
as she was strong enough to do so.

She tried to explain her motives to
Eliza Bennett, but though the servant
was afraid (in consequence) to show all the
sympathy she felt for her young mistress,
she could not approve of the harshness
Mrs Barrington displayed towards her.
She often attempted to stand between the
mother and daughter on the occasion of
those sad quarrels, which had made
themselves patent to the ears of Sainte
Pauvrette; but she found that her inter-

ference only made matters worse, and her best plan was to preserve neutrality.

One terrible night, however, when the frosts of December and January had covered the country with a pall of white, and the snow lay several feet deep in the lower parts of the village, an alter-cation—which commenced (on Mrs Bar-rington's part) with covert sneers and words of contempt, and culminated in loud tones of anger and several smart blows—had nearly proved the end of poor Fenella's troubles.

She stood before her mother, half fainting from fear, and without a word to say in self-defence, until the indig-nities offered her, and the abuse cast upon one whom (though unnamed) she could not hear reviled with impunity, sent all the blood in her body rushing to her brain, and deprived her of the mastery over her senses. With a loud cry to God for mercy, and before Mrs Barrington (being alone) could prevent

the action, Fenella had flown bareheaded
from the house, and flung herself into
a sluggish stream, half ice and half water,
which ran in front of it.

Then Mrs Barrington was thoroughly
alarmed, and screamed to Eliza Bennett for
assistance; and all the neighbours were
roused by the disturbance, and brought
lanterns and lighted pine torches to help
in the search.

They had not to go far. The senseless
figure of Fenella was soon found—thrown
violently across the mixture of ice and
muddy water of which the winter stream
was composed; and being wrapped up in
a blanket by Bennett, was carried back to
the house and placed in bed. But the
inhabitants of Sainte Pauvrette had plenty
to say of the occurrence afterwards, and
Madame Jeanne was not backward in
giving her opinion on the matter.

'Did I not tell you what that Englishwoman was?' she exclaimed next day,
when it was openly announced in the

village that the poor young lady was lying
dangerously ill of a brain fever. 'A pig!
a devil! for all the fine yellow curls that
she keeps in a box, and the pretty pink
colour she would have us believe to be her
own! She has used that poor *demoiselle*
shamefully ever since she came here, and
now she wants to kill her—that is my
belief! Else why does not she have a
doctor to see her in this fever; and why
has she sent away the ogre, Mademoiselle
Elise, just when she wants her help most?
Oh, but you need not stare at me in
that manner! I only tell the truth, and
Madame Regnier cannot deny it, although
she *is* so anxious to make out her tenant
to be everything that is good. Mademoiselle the ogre left Sainte Pauvrette this
morning by ten o'clock. I met her walking on the road to Arniers to catch the
diligence, with her large basket on her
arm; and when I asked her the reason
of her journey, she replied she had business to do for her mistress in Arniers.

But she has not returned, *mes dames*—she
has not returned; and meanwhile *la belle
petite* lies in bed with an attack of the
brain, and no doctor is sent for to attend
her; and Collette, who has been engaged
to do their housework, is not permitted to
go into the room, of which the door is
kept locked by her mother. But if she
dies,' continued Madame Jeanne, with a
threatening shake of the head,—'if that
beautiful young lady dies, without help or
assistance, and after all the cruelty she has
been subjected to, *I* shall say it is murder,
for one—let who will be the other.'

Meanwhile what the irate hotel-keeper
said was true. Eliza Bennett had gone
that morning to Arniers; more, she had
crossed to England. She and her mistress
had been closeted all night with the unfortunate girl who had been rescued from the
mud and the ice, and who only returned to
consciousness to fall into a burning fever,
and rave deliriously of the troubles which
had occasioned it.

'This is the climax,' said Mrs Barrington, with a look of despair, and as if the
climax had not been in a great measure
brought on by herself. 'We must lock the
door of her room, Bennett, and let no one
but ourselves pass in and out. She talks
in French, and I would not have these
ignorant creatures overhear what she says
for any mortal consideration.'

The two women consulted long and
earnestly on what was best to be done in
the matter ; and when the morning dawned,
the key unturned in the lock of Fenella's
door, and Eliza Bennett, creeping out of
it, with a white and troubled face, went
up to her own room, and attired herself in
her walking things.

In the space of a few minutes her mistress followed her, with a large basket on
her arm.

'You will travel as quickly as ever you
can,' she said, as she placed some money
in her hands, 'and return to us as soon
as possible. This fever is sure to abate

in a few hours, and I shall not keep
Fenella here one day longer than is
absolutely necessary.'

'Return to you, my dear mistress!'
exclaimed the servant; 'why, what else
should I do? Am I not taking this
journey entirely for your sake and that of
the dear child! Keep her as cool as
possible, ma'am, and don't let her have
anything but slops and fever drinks till
I come back. I will be with you at the
end of a week again, without fail.'

Mrs Barrington sat down and began
to cry feebly.

'I don't know what I shall do without
you,' she wailed; 'it's horrible to sit and
listen to her ravings and reproaches; but
I am sure it is best that you should go
to England at once, and then the business
will be over. But you are a dear, good,
valuable creature Bennett, and I shall count
the minutes till you come back again.'

She kissed the servant on both cheeks
as she spoke, and Eliza Bennett went on

her way rejoicing. She crossed to Dover
the same day, and was at Ines-cedwyn
by the following evening. It was evident
that the business she had been entrusted
to transact for her mistress was, in some
manner, concerned with her brother Benjamin, and the place where Fenella had
made that fatal acquaintance in the ruined
bungalow, which brought ill-luck to all
who meddled with it. There was no
necessity for Eliza Bennett to remain in
Ines-cedwyn after she had obtained the
information which she came to seek. She
was anxious to rejoin her mistress, and
the associations of her birthplace had become distasteful to her.

She had adhered faithfully, however,
to the business upon which Mrs Barrington had sent her to England, and
been careful not to say a word about her
young lady's illness, or the cause. She
was, therefore, considerably startled the
next morning, as she was preparing to
leave the cottage, to hear Martha say,—

' By the way, 'Liza, do you remember the talk as there was here last summer about Miss Fenella having got a beau? Well, I expect that young feller's bin hangin' about here again in hopes of gettin' another sight of 'er. *I* don't know 'im, of course, no more than Adam, but Tugwell the boatman says he has met 'im several times in Lynwern; and the day before yesterday, when I came back from Freshpool (where I had gone about some eggs), my servant girl told me as a gentleman had called to see me, and seemed quite put out like by my being from home. He was a fine-lookin' feller too, the girl says—tall and 'ansome; and it may have been 'im, and it may not, but it seems likely—now don't it?'

Eliza Bennett turned white and red under this exordium, as if she had been accused of having a '*beau*' herself.

' It ain't of much consequence one way or the other,' she replied, trying to speak indifferently; ' my young lady looks higher than that comes to. You don't suppose she would think twice of a beau as she picked up on the Ines-cedwyn sands?'

'Lor', no! in course not; only I thought I might as well mention it to you. Well, good-bye, 'Liza, and thank you for thinking of us in this matter, and thank your mistress, too, for· .the recommendation. And I shall hear from the parties, I suppose, in a few days. I'm glad to have 'ad this peep at you, though you don't look over and above well, to my mind; but I 'opes you'll get over safe to your ladies, and that it won't be long afore you're all back in England again.'

'Oh yes! we shall be home in the summer, never fear! Good-bye to you, Martha,' said Eliza Bennett, as she set off to walk to Lynwern.

She plodded along the country road, over ruts hardened by the ice and snow, with her head bent down upon her bosom, and her mind filled with her sister-in-law's communication.

'I'd like to catch him hangin' about any place as *we* was in,' she thought indignantly; '*I'd* let 'im know what was what —the dirty, mean, sneaking scoundrel, to go and leave a poor girl in that way, and cause us all this misery! I only wish I had the handling of him! *I'd* make him pay for his whistle.'

She was so absorbed in her dreams of revenge that she stumbled up against some one in the road, before her brother Benjamin's cottage was out of sight, and had to draw back with a demand for pardon.

'It is of no consequence,' replied a sweet, grave voice; 'but I think I am speaking to Mrs Bennett, am I not?'

The woman looked up quickly. Before her stood a gentleman—young, handsome, tall and upright—a gentleman whom she had never seen before except by the uncertain light of the moon, but whom she recognised at once. It was, in fact, Geoffrey Doyne; and so great in the magic of

beauty, and a superior station, and another
sex, that, as Eliza Bennett looked at him,
all her deep-laid plans of revenge melted
into thin air.

'No, sir,' she answered, in a voice that
palpably trembled, 'I am not *Mrs* Bennett;
I am her sister-in-law, Eliza Bennett.'

'*Eliza Bennett!*' he repeated quickly;
'is it possible? Are you the person—the
maid—that accompanied a young lady
down to Ines-cedwyn last summer?'

'Yes, sir, I am,' said Eliza stoutly.
('He's very handsome, the villin!' she
thought to herself, 'and he's got a win-
ning way with his tongue, drat it! but he
sha'n't get any information of her where-
abouts out of me—not if he was to drag
me at the tail of four wild 'orses.')

'Oh! then you can tell me where she
is?' exclaimed Geoffrey Doyne excitedly.
'Give me her address, I beg of you, in
Heaven's name! I have a particular—
a *very* particular reason for wishing to
obtain it.'

The servant looked him full in the face.

'And I may have a particular reason, sir, for wishing to keep it from you ; for, if I'm not greatly mistaken, you are the same gentleman that used to meet my young lady down on the sands here last summer.'

Geoffrey Doyne's eyes fell before hers.

'Yes,' he answered, in a low voice, 'I am the same.'

'Well, may God forgive you for it,' said the woman, 'for *I* can't. You've ruined her life as surely as ever a man ruined a woman ! And I brought her up from a baby ; she is like my own child to me. You might as well have killed me at the same time ; I couldn't have felt it more,' and Eliza Bennett caught up her woollen shawl to wipe away two large tears that were rolling down her cheeks.

At her words Geoffrey Doyne became pallid with fear.

'Killed her ! ruined her !' he repeated vehemently, as he caught the servant by

the arm; 'in God's name tell me what
you mean! Is she ill — is she dead?
What have I done? If you don't put me
out of this suspense, I shall go mad!'

They were just opposite the Beach
Bungalow as he spoke. Eliza Bennett
glanced at it significantly.

'Come in here, sir,' she said,—'I don't
want the whole village to hear what I've
got to say to you—and I'll tell you what
you've done.'

She led the way into the ruined villa,
and Geoffrey Doyne followed her, sick at
heart with remorse and apprehension.

'May I make so bold, sir,' began Eliza
Bennett, as soon as they were sheltered
from observation, 'as to ask if—so be
—you're married?'

'Yes!' he replied; 'I am.'

'And what's the good, then, of your
hanging about Ines-cedwyn to try and
see my young lady? What could you
say to her—how could you look at her,
if you did meet?'

'Oh, I don't know—I cannot tell!' he exclaimed wildly. 'Only the separation, the silence, the want of seeing her is more than I can bear. If you will only tell me where she is, or take a letter to her, that I may have one word of kind- ness, one word of pardon in reply, I fancy I could bear the rest with fortitude. Mrs Bennett, I ought to have gone back to India long ago. My leave was up in the autumn, but I got an extension, only for this — to find out her address and see her once before I go. Then I will leave England and trouble her no more.'

'You will never get your wish through me, sir,' said Eliza Bennett, 'for I'll neither tell you where she is, nor carry any notes between you. You've done her enough mischief already, and you've put it out of your power to do her any good. The best thing you can do now, for her and yourself, is never to write to her nor see her any more.'

'But does she ever speak of me? Does she remember me?' he demanded eagerly.

'*Remember* you!' echoed the servant, in a tone of contempt. 'I should think you'd given her enough cause to remember you, in this life and the next too! But there are different sorts of remembrance, sir, and if my young mistress is the lady I take her for, her best remembrance of you will be one of hatred and of scorn!'

'I deserve it,' he answered brokenly.

'And so you do,' said Bennett, with the want of delicacy that usually characterises her class, 'and so you'll say twice over when you've heard what I've got to tell you.'

And thereupon she gave him an account of Fenella's mental and bodily sufferings during the autumn and winter, sparing no detail that might add to the colouring of the picture, and winding up with a description of her attempt at self-destruction, and the brain fever that had succeeded it.

'And now, what do you think of yourself, sir?' she said, as she concluded. 'You're a nice sort of gentleman, aren't you, to ask me to carry notes to that poor suffering angel, and rake up all her troubles afresh, just as she has a chance maybe of getting over them. We'd never have known your *name* even, if it hadn't been for her delirious ravings; but we sha'n't forget it in a hurry, you may take your oath of that! And don't you attempt to come nigh her again, sir—not for the rest of your mortal life, —for I do believe her mamma would tear you limb from limb if you did.'

Geoffrey Doyne during her relation had shown every symptom of the deepest feeling. His brow had flushed darkly with shame, his nostrils had quivered, his lips grown white, his whole frame shaken with emotion. And now that it was concluded, all he seemed able to

do was to lean against the window-sill,
whilst the words, '*My God! my God!*'
seemed to be wrung from the very depths
of his tortured heart. His suffering was
so self-evident that even Eliza Bennett
could not help pitying him.

'Don't take on like that, sir,' she said
soothingly; 'it won't mend the past,
and the best thing we can all do now
is to try and forget it. I don't know,
I'm sure, as I've done right to tell you
so much; but it'll be safe with you,
and I thought as you ought to know
what my young lady has gone through.
Maybe it will save others, for you gentlemen don't seem to stand at nothing
when you've set your mind upon a thing.
But I didn't mean to upset you like
this, sir, and I beg your pardon if I've
gone too far.'

'No, no! I should wish to have
known it,' he said huskily; and then he
pulled out several pieces of gold from
his waistcoat-pocket, and tried to thrust

them in her hand. But she put them back again proudly.

'No, Mr Doyne. I couldn't take *your* money, thank you; not even if I'd done anything to deserve it, which I haven't. But I hope you'll give me your promise before you go never to try and write to Miss Fenella again. Don't make the harm you've done, worse, sir. You've got your own lady to consider and to look after now, and you can't do no good to mine! Will you promise me this?'

'Yes—I promise!' he said, in a broken voice.

'And please not to walk alongside of me to Lynwern either, sir! Meeting of you has upset me more than I care to think of, and I'd like to be alone for the rest of the journey.'

'I will respect your wishes,' replied Geoffrey Doyne quickly; and then, raising his hat, as if she had been his equal, he left the ruined bungalow, and strode along the cliffs in the opposite direction to Lynwern.

Eliza Bennett looked after him for a few moments before she pursued her own way.

'Well, he may be a villin, but he's a fine-looking gentleman,' she thought as she dried her eyes, 'and they would have made a handsome couple. What a thousand pities it is that Miss Fenella couldn't have him. But there! it's always the way in this world. Them as ought to come together, don't; and them as 'ates each other like poison, is tied for life. The more I sees of marriage, the more thankful I am as I was never tempted into it!'

She pursued her road to Lynwern after this, and proceeded on her journey back to Sainte Pauvrette. And a few hours later Geoffrey Doyne followed her to London, and walked into the presence of his wife. They were living at an hotel, preparatory to going back to India. There was no lack of love on the part of Mrs Geoffrey

Doyne towards her husband, and (except when dark thoughts of Fenella Barrington interposed between them) he usually returned her ebullitions of affection with a certain degree of interest. It is difficult for a young and ardent nature not to evince some feeling when clasped in the arms of a pretty woman who has every right to expect an adequate return. And Geoffrey Doyne had a very affectionate disposition. His fault was that he loved too much, not too little. He was passionate, moreover, and easily moved; and to be caressed, and flattered, and made much of, was almost a necessity to him. But on this occasion his wife found all her artifices to attract his notice, failures. He had been absent nearly a week, on some business of which she had not the faintest idea; and yet when he returned home, instead of being glad to see her again, and anxious to hear what she had been doing in his absence, he was morose, gloomy, and

dejected, complained of every dish that
appeared on the dinner-table, and scarcely
spoke a dozen words to her during the
evening. Had she indulged his mood
and left him to himself, she would have
been rewarded by seeing the cloud gradu-
ally pass away (at all events, to outward
view), but Jessie did not understand how
to treat her husband.

That phantom of a former love, which
he had once mentioned to her, was ever
coming between them now, and she was
always quick to ascribe his varying moods
to regret that he had married her. For
six months they had been husband and
wife, but they were no nearer each other
in love or confidence or friendship than
they had been at first. Geoffrey accepted
her attentions to him, and that was all.

Women are very apt to imagine that
the possession of the beloved object is
everything, and that they can bear the
idea of a rival better if they know him
to be, beyond all dispute, their own.

They too often live to find out they have
deceived themselves. To be married to
a person you love, but who does not
love you, is very much like trying to
grasp a bubble—each time your fingers
close upon it you will find them still
unsatisfied and empty.

'What is the matter, Geoffrey?' demanded Jessie, as he thrust away the
wine decanters and leant back moodily
in his chair. 'I never saw any one so
disagreeable as you have made yourself
to-night. If this is the effect of having
a holiday, I should say you had better
remain at home for the future. Where
have you been?'

'It would not interest you to know,'
Geoffrey.

'Oh, that is as good as saying that you
don't intend to tell me! just as when you
receive a letter and put it into your pocket
without showing it to me, and declare it is
on business that I can't understand.'

'Perhaps it is!'

'But I have a right to ask where you've been, and whom you've seen, Geoffrey: and if you refuse to tell me, I shall think the very worst.'

'That will only hurt yourself, Jessie. Aren't you content with having married me, with knowing that, wherever I go, you have a right to demand to follow? And can't you let me enjoy a few hours' liberty without pestering to ascertain exactly where I have spent them?'

'No, I can't! because I always suspect you go where that other girl lives (the girl you told me of, you remember); and I always *shall* suspect it when you go away alone in this mysterious manner, as long as ever I live. I know when you are thinking of her, too—when you pucker up your eyebrows, Geoffrey, and look gloomy, and speak in that horrible cross way; and you make me miserable—you know you do.'

'You make yourself miserable, you mean. However, if what you say is true, don't recall her memory by mentioning the subject. I have already told you it is an unpleasant one to me.'

'Oh yes! because you wish you had married her instead of me; and you get wretched when you think of it. But it is most unfair of you to go and see her, behind my back; and everybody would say the same.'

'I have not been to see her,' replied Geoffrey, with visible annoyance.

'But you think of her — you cannot deny it.'

'Yes, I *do* think of her! A man has. not absolute control over his thoughts.'

'A pretty confession for a married man to make!' pouted Jessie. 'Why don't you follow it up by saying that you love her still?'

The young man was fairly roused by this time.

'I don't deny it,' he answered petulantly. 'I do love her still.'

'And I suppose you'll end by running

away with her, and leaving me to go back
to papa in Blenheim Square! It is shame-
ful, scandalous! and she must be a wicked,
vile creature to encourage you to forget
your duty in this way.'

Geoffrey Doyne rose from his chair, and
struck his hand upon the table with a force
that made the glasses ring.

'Don't you dare to speak of her in such
terms before me,' he said angrily. 'She
is no more vile nor wicked than yourself.
She is as pure and good a girl as ever
walked God's earth, and you are the only
person on whom there is any necessity to
call "shame." You chose to hold me to
my promise of marriage, when you knew
that my heart was no longer mine to give
you; and, therefore, the consequences
must be on your own head. I *do* love
that girl you mention, earnestly, faithfully,
affectionately, and I *shall* love her to my
life's end. There! you wished for the
truth, and you have it. You exacted the
payment of my bond to the last ounce of

flesh. But you can't have the blood, Jessie—*my heart's blood.* That belongs to another, and ever will do so. And now, if you wish to preserve the peace, you will drop this subject once and for ever, as it can never raise anything but strife between us.'

This was all the satisfaction that she obtained from him, and a few weeks after they were on their way together to rejoin his regiment in India.

About the same time Eliza Bennett led Fenella out for her first walk in the open air. The girl, although much pulled down by her illness, was on the high road to recovery, but she did not appear to have regained her spirits with her strength. The little Wallon children ran out of the cottages as she passed, with bunches of violets and primroses in their hands, and Fenella smiled sweetly at them as she accepted their offerings. But the smile was as sad as ever, and the grey eyes still looked wistful and scared; and as, accompanied by her nurse, she dragged her steps up to the little churchyard, the peasant women shook their heads at one another, and said she would be carried there yet.

'You mustn't sit down, my dear,' said Eliza Bennett; 'it's too cold for that yet. But you've done bravely for a first attempt, and we shall have you stout and strong upon your legs again before many days is past. You will try and leave off fretting now, my dear young lady, won't you? for your own sake, and your mamma's, and all as love you.'

'Oh yes, nurse, I will try.'

'It's no use crying over spilt milk, Miss Fenella, and you're too young and pretty to have your whole life wasted for a first mistake. You must try and look at what's past in a sensible light, my dear; and you'll live to laugh over these times, I warrant you.'

The girl shivered, but she answered in the same words as before.

'Yes, nurse, I will try.'

Then Bennett lowered her voice.

'Miss Fenella dear, you won't mind
what I'm going to say, but I couldn't
help guessing his name on account of
your raving after him so in your illness,
and when I was in London the other
day about some money business of your
mamma's, I made a few inquiries—secret
like—about him, and he's gone, my dear.
He's left England for good and all, and
you won't never see him, nor be troubled
with him again ; and that ought to be
as great a comfort to you as anything
else—oughtn't it, now ?'

The blood had ebbed and flowed in
Fenella's wasted cheeks, as Bennett
spoke to her, like waves of white and
crimson, and when the servant turned
for an answer, she saw a bright hectic
spot burning under each of her eyes.
But the tone in which she spoke was
very calm and deliberate.

'Thank you, nurse,' she said wearily.

'You meant it kindly, I know, but nothing
is of any consequence to me now. Only,
please remember (and I am sure you
will, for my sake) that I would rather not
hear you mention his name again. He
is dead to me, nurse; I am dead; everything seems dead together. Don't forget
that, and never speak to me on the subject more! And now take me home;
I have made myself worse by coming
here; the sooner my mother takes me
away from Sainte Pauvrette the better.'

She cast the violets and primroses upon
the grave by which she had been standing
as she spoke, and then throwing her arm
about Bennett's neck, turned from the
spot without another word.

CHAPTER V.

SIR GILBERT CONROY.

'He that hath nature in him must be grateful,
'Tis the Creator's primary great law.'

Madan.

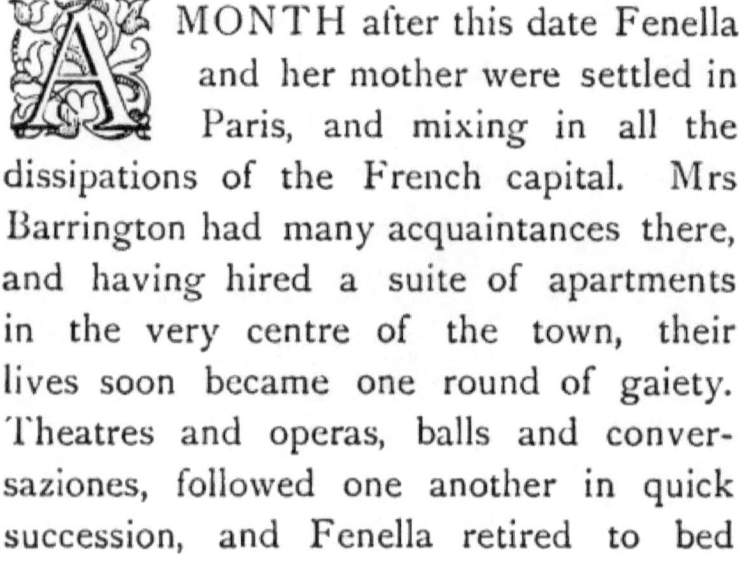

A MONTH after this date Fenella and her mother were settled in Paris, and mixing in all the dissipations of the French capital. Mrs Barrington had many acquaintances there, and having hired a suite of apartments in the very centre of the town, their lives soon became one round of gaiety. Theatres and operas, balls and conversaziones, followed one another in quick succession, and Fenella retired to bed

each night almost too weary to think.
It was good for her, and it would be
untrue to say that she did not, in a
measure, enjoy the change. To depict
either a man or a woman as brooding
incessantly over their trouble, and never
for a moment losing sight of it, to raise
cheerful eyes to the light of Heaven,
would be utterly unnatural. No one ever
did so in this world and preserved his
senses. The strain upon the nerves would
be too great, and the mind would break
down beneath it. Fenella often returned
from the gay scenes into which her mother
took her, to think how much more she
would have enjoyed them had Geoffrey
Doyne not proved unfaithful, and sob
herself to sleep over the remembrance.
Yet, whilst she was mixing in them, they
distracted her thoughts, and drew her out
of herself. The theatre was a wondrous
revelation to her; the opera, a sublime
delight; even at the balls and assemblies
she began to take pleasure in the know-

ledge that she was admired, and that all men did not consider her so worthless a thing that they could take her up, and cast her aside, as the humour seized them.

Mrs Barrington had shown wisdom in her generation in making her daughter's sojourn in Sainte Pauvrette a time which she shuddered to recall. Anything which would expunge that terrible remembrance from her mind would have been welcome to Fenella; it may be supposed, then, how gladly she hailed the fresh scenes which opened before her, and how gratefully she accepted the salve they offered to her wounded vanity. For we are all mortal, and there is no doubt that trouble is easier to bear when we have less time to think about it. And it is well it is so, else the world would be full of lunatics and suicides. The man who receives a bullet during the heat of battle in his body, which the surgeons are unable to extract, will feel its presence to the last day of his life, and at some times more than at others. A change in the weather or a derangement of his system will cause the pain to be as acute as on the day he was shot; and yet when the sun shines, and his blood is free from acid, he may go for months without remembering he ever encountered such an accident. So it is with our hearts. The mercy of God and the goodness of friends may dull the sense of injury or loss for months together, but it never totally disappears. If a lesser grief overtakes us, a lesser love becomes estranged, the old wound opens and bleeds afresh, the bullet stirs in the flesh, and we recognise the fact that we are maimed for life. Let us not grudge the wounded, then, their moments of forgetfulness, nor ridicule the trifles which may have the power to divert their thoughts.

To an older person, perhaps, white satin and pearls might appear an unworthy panacea for a disappointed affection; but to a young creature like

Fenella, who had never possessed anything but serge and cotton frocks before,
they held their charm. She sighed, it
is true, when she saw the pale loveliness, which Bennett had taken such
pains to adorn, reflected in the looking-
glass, and wondered, if Geoffrey could
have seen her like that, if he would
ever have forsaken her. Still, she preferred to be handsome rather than ugly,
and could take a pride in her personal
appearance, though her lover was not
there to praise it. It was natural that
she should do so, and it is of no use
crying out against nature.

But there was one thing in which
Fenella's faith had been utterly destroyed and could never be built up
again, and that was her mother's love
for her. Mrs Barrington would have
had it otherwise. When she found that
her daughter's beauty had not been destroyed by her illness—that she was,
in fact, better looking than she had

been before, and that she made no
objection to going out to dances and
theatres every night, and wearing any
sort of costume which was provided for
her, Mrs Barrington's good temper
began to revive, and she would have
had Fenella share her rouge and powder
and her hare's-foot, and forget all old
injuries. But the girl was unable to
do so. About the past she was as
silent as the grave. She never mentioned Geoffrey Doyne, nor Ines-cedwyn,
nor Sainte Pauvrette ; but to blot out
the memory of them was impossible.
She could not forget her mother's
harshness and cruelty, nor the sneers
and contempt cast upon her when her
heart was bleeding for one word of
affection or sympathy. She saw Mrs
Barrington in her true colours—worldly,
selfish, and deceitful ; and as long as
she lived, Fenella could never set her
up again on the pedestal her childish
enthusiasm had raised for her. She

accepted her caresses without any exhi-
bition of dislike; she thanked her for
her compliments, and followed her
wishes; but here the link between
them ended. Mrs Barrington had
brought her into the world, certainly;
but Fenella, remembering Sainte Pauvrette, could never again think of her
as her *mother.*

The word 'mother' is sacred. It
holds within its couple of syllables a
host of loving possibilities; and the
woman who cannot sympathise with
every pulsation of the life she gave, is
not worthy of the name.

Fenella put the thought resolutely
from her—it was only another trouble
added to the load she bore—and tried
to believe that the sweet dream she had
once cherished was of a mother who
had died when she was born.

Mrs Barrington was her adviser, and
protector, and chaperon—everything that
was needful in the world of fashion she

had entered, but something which she never wished to encounter when alone. At such times, a suspicious reserve and awkwardness would fall upon both mother and daughter, which warned them to make the interview as short as possible.

Mrs Barrington, however, was quite in her element again. Her ambitious views for Fenella had all revived (though she did not like to say too much about them to the girl herself), and she spared no pains nor expense to render her as attractive as she possibly could.

The pale loveliness of the English girl, which owed so much to her lofty bearing and look of serious innocence, soon began to be talked of in the Parisian *salons*, and more than one man of fashion was said to be a suitor for her hand.

But Mrs Barrington was very cautious who she admitted as a visitor to her own house. She had no intention of marrying Fenella to a penniless *attaché*, or an officer dependent on his pay. She wanted to secure both a title and a fortune for her daughter, and the only admirer she had who combined these advantages was her own old acquaintance, Sir Gilbert Conroy.

Time had been—and not so very long ago either — when the fair widow had hoped to get Sir Gilbert for herself, but her chances had never had any existence except in her own brain, and she was sensible enough to perceive that, if she snubbed his advances to Fenella, he was not likely to ask for her mother's hand instead. Besides, the baronet's suit had great advantages. He was not a hot-headed boy, determined to have his own way at all hazards, and run the risk of a refusal by speaking too soon. He rather preferred the dignified old fashion of consulting the parents or guardians of the young lady he desired to make his wife, before he mentioned the subject to herself. And Mrs Barrington preferred this method of courtship also.

She knew Fenella's impulsive temperament, and her love of truth and honour; and she was terribly afraid of what her daughter might say to any young man who addressed her on the subject of marriage. If the preliminary matters were kept in *her* hands, she felt that she could smooth down any little unpleasantnesses that may have occurred in the past, so as to make them appear rather desirable experiences for a young woman than otherwise.

Sir Gilbert Conroy was a gentleman in every sense of the word. He was a man of birth and education, of almost courtly breeding and ultra-refinement. In age he was about five-and-thirty; in appearance he was fair and aristocratic, with hair cropped closely to his head, and rather bald about the temples, where he brushed it backwards; with a handsome nose, quiet blue eyes, and a thin-lipped mouth shaded by a small moustache. He was a man whom any woman might have

been proud to be connected with—but
he was a man who would be severe
in his judgments, and unforgiving where
he was offended.

He had been struck with Fenella Barrington on the first occasion of their meeting at an embassy ball, and had assiduously followed up the acquaintance since.
And the girl liked him—not with any
idea of marriage (she had conceived a
notion that it was impossible she could
ever marry now), but as a pleasant
acquaintance, who could talk more sen-
sibly than the generality of men, and who
always seemed delighted to meet her,
and proud to be her partner for the
evening !

But when Mrs Barrington first mentioned the possibility of her marrying
Sir Gilbert Conroy, Fenella felt as if
she had been struck with a sudden blow.
It was the morning after they had attended a large party at the house of the
Russian ambassador, and Eliza Bennett

announced to her young lady that coffee was waiting for her in her mamma's dressing-room.

'The mistress is too tired to go downstairs, Miss Fenella; so she says, please will you go in and take it with her there.'

The girl threw on her *robe de chambre*, and obeyed the summons. Her cheeks were flushed from sleep; her eyes were languid; her fair hair hung in two thick plaits down her back.

'Really, child,' exclaimed Mrs Barrington, as she entered, 'you grow handsomer every day. It's no wonder Sir Gilbert is making such a fool of himself about you.'

Fenella laughed.

'Poor Sir Gilbert! Why is he to be called a fool for liking me, more than any one else?'

'Because he likes you more than any one else does. Surely, Fenella, you are not so blind as not to see that!'

The girl opened her eyes.

'Does he ?   I hope not !'

'And why so, my dear ?   Most young ladies would be proud of his preference. His title is one of the oldest baronetcies in England, and he has five thousand a-year on which to keep it up.'

'Oh, I don't mean that, mamma; I am aware he is rich ; only—you know—it would be of no use his liking me, because I could never marry him—nor anyone !   So I hope it is all fancy on your part.'

'What nonsense, Fenella.   You must put such fantastical ideas out of your head.   And as for its being my fancy that Sir Gilbert likes you, he has already asked my consent to his proposing for your hand.'

Fenella grew scarlet.

' Oh, mamma, did you tell him ?'

'What ?' cried Mrs Barrington sharply.

'About — about — what has happened, you know.'

'Am I a born fool, or an idiot?'
exclaimed her mother. 'No! *of course*
I didn't tell him! What are you thinking of, Fenella?'

'Forgive me, mamma! I ought to
have known without asking. You would
not tell him, naturally, for my sake as
well as your own. But what did you
say, then?'

'I told him he had my heartiest wishes
for his success, and he might propose to
you whenever he liked.'

Fenella's distress was genuine.

'Oh, mamma, why did you do that,
when you know I can have but one
answer to give him? I *couldn't* marry
him even if I liked him. How could I?
You might have saved me from the
ordeal of having to tell him so.'

'But you must tell him no such thing,
Fenella, and I will not allow you to see
Sir Gilbert again until I have talked you
into a more sensible frame of mind. Now,
my dear, do try and look at the matter in

a reasonable light. You *must* marry ; you know that !'

'No, indeed I don't. I never intend to marry. I have given up all thoughts of it—once and for ever.'

'And how do you suppose I am to support you, then ?' exclaimed her mother. 'Do you think I have sufficient money to maintain a household, and provide you with dresses, and take you about to places of amusement, for the remainder of your life ?'

Fenella stared.

'Yes, I thought so, mamma. Haven't we money ? Didn't papa leave any behind him ?'

'*Your papa !*' repeated Mrs Barrington witheringly. 'A fine provision he left us ! The pension for a post-captain's widow, and a few thousands in the bank. Why, I spent that to the last farthing ages ago, and have nothing but my pension at the present time. I am going in debt for every mortal thing we use, and eat, and wear. And then you sit there and tell me

calmly that you never intend to marry!
Why, it's flying in the face of Providence;
it's condemning us both to perpetual
poverty, and your mother to losing everything she possesses; for if I can't pay
my bills, my creditors will certainly put in
a distraint upon the furniture in South
Audley Street.'

'Oh, mamma! mamma! why didn't
you tell me of this long ago? Why have
you dressed me up in expensive clothes,
and taken me to all these fine places, when
you could not afford it? I would rather
have gone in sackcloth and eaten dry bread,
than run you into such terrible difficulties!'

'Why have I done it, Fenella?' replied Mrs Barrington. 'Why, to procure
you the very chance which you declare
you shall throw away—to see you suitably
married, and placed above the reach of
poverty and care.'

'But how *can* I, mamma? Answer
the question yourself. How *can* I?'
said Fenella pleadingly.

'I suppose I can guess what you are alluding to,' replied her mother coldly; 'but if you intend to let that foolish love affair stand in the way of your future prospects, all I can say is that you will be intensely selfish. Most people would think you had caused me sufficient trouble and anxiety already, without making more. If you are really sorry for what is past, Fenella, now is your time to redeem it. You will never have a better chance.'

'Oh, I *am* sorry,' returned the girl, with troubled eyes and clasped hands; 'God knows I am! But how can I remedy it? You know my heart is broken, mother; that my whole life is spoiled. What man would marry me now, if he knew the truth?'

'No one, of course! Very few men would marry at all if they knew the truth about the women they make their wives. But who do you suppose will tell Sir Gilbert Conroy anything? I sha'n't— you may take your oath of that; and

our dear good Bennett is as secret as the
grave. There is no fear of his ever knowing the truth. You may set your mind
entirely at rest on that point.'

' But I wouldn't accept him unless he
knew it,' said Fenella. ' Mamma, what do
you take me for ? Do you think I could
be so false, so dishonourable as that ? '

Mrs Barrington wheeled round in her
chair and regarded her daughter with the
utmost astonishment.

' Fenella,' she said solemnly, ' you're a
born fool, and where you get it from beats
my comprehension. If you are going to
enter into marriage with the idea of telling
your husband everything that has ever
happened to you, or that ever will happen
to you, you may dismiss at once the idea
of having any peace in your life. Why, if
the world were conducted on that plan, it
would be a perfect volcano ! Now, I have
seen a great deal more of it than you have,
and you must allow yourself to be guided
by me. Your husband will never tell you

any more about his own affairs than he chooses, you may make up your mind to that ; and the less you tell him about your-self the better.'

But Mrs Barrington's worldly wisdom had no effect upon the frank and generous mind of her daughter.

'Mamma,' she said, 'if I marry Sir Gilbert Conroy, or anybody else, you know that I can never love him.   I might learn to be grateful for his kind-ness to me, but my heart is gone.   I don't think I've got any heart left.   I feel as if the place where it ought to be was empty.'

'That's nonsense, my dear,' said her mother impatiently.   'We are all like that when we're young.   We have a first love, and we fancy we can never love again ; and after a while we find the diffi-culty is to keep ourselves from loving too much.   And even if it were not the case, it's no good carrying that enthusiastic, gushing sort of feeling into marriage.   It worries a man to death, and wears out his affection sooner than anything else. Never refuse any attention your husband may wish to show you, but keep your own feelings within bounds. That is the secret of a happy marriage, and you will find a man will care all the more for you if there is a little indifference and reserve on your part.'

Fenella sighed. Her idea of a happy marriage had been so very different from that.

'But if it is unnecessary to give love to the man you marry, mamma,' she answered, 'is it not all the more incumbent to be perfectly open with him? And I could not live my life with a secret always weighing at my heart. I should fancy each time he frowned at me that he was going to tell me he had discovered I was false to him.'

'Oh, well, if you are determined to stand in your own light and mine, and take no advice from those who know

better than yourself, there is no more to
be said on the subject,' replied Mrs Barrington, with the air of a martyr; 'but
I must say that it is hard upon me—
bitterly, cruelly hard.'

'Oh, how can I help you?' cried the
girl. 'What can I do to remedy the
evil I have brought upon us both?'

'The only thing you can do, you refuse to do,' said her mother, reproach-
fully.

'I cannot do a dishonourable action,'
replied Fenella, with dignity.

And after that conclusion they passed
several days in a miserable state of cold-
ness and silence towards each other.

Mrs Barrington confided the whole
affair to Bennett, and implored her to
argue it out with Fenella. For the
sympathy she had displayed during her
illness had drawn the girl and the old
woman very closely together. Indeed,
Bennett may be said to have been the
only real friend Fenella had; and many

a time since those miserable days had
she cried herself to sleep upon the servant's bosom. So it seemed nothing
more than natural when Bennett said to
her,—

'Why have you made your mamma
so angry with you, Miss Fenella? What
is it that you don't like in Sir Gilbert
Conroy?'

'I like him well enough, Bennett,' said
the girl, with a sigh. 'In fact, I see
nothing to dislike in him. Only that
has nothing to do with marriage, you
know; and mamma can't understand that
it is impossible for me to forget.'

'But it's your *duty* to forget, my dear,'
replied Bennett, who was brushing Fenella's hair at the time. 'Here's Sir
Gilbert Conroy, a fine, handsome gentleman, with plenty of money to keep you
comfortable and give you everything you
want, and dying to make you his lady,
and yet you won't listen to a word he
says. And all because of a business as

can never come to anything.   For, you
see, there's where it is, Miss Fenella.
If there was any hope or probability
like of things turning out as you would
wish them, there might be some sense
in waiting ; but you know as there isn't.
And when all's said and done, my dear,
the first wasn't a patch upon Sir Gilbert.'

'*Don't*, nurse—*don't*,' murmured Fenella, in a voice of pain, as her hands
went up to shade her blinded eyes.   Ah !
that First!   Let a dozen come after him
—fairer, better, and more true than he
—but they will never have the power
to drive his image from the heart that
sheltered it.

The nurse laid down her brush, and
kissed the crown of the fair head that
was bowed upon the dressing-table.

' There — there, my lamb,' she said
affectionately ; ' I wish I had bit out
my tongue afore I'd said them words.
But it was for the sake of your mamma,

Miss Fenella. She's regular put out, my dear; and no wonder, for she quite counted on your marriage as a means of righting herself, and I'm afraid she'll be in a terrible fix if you continue to set your face against it.'

Fenella looked up suddenly.

'Bennett, tell me the truth,' she said. 'Are we so very poor? is mamma really in want of money?' ·

'Indeed she is, miss. Don't you remember my telling you at the convent a year ago, that your dear mamma was full of troubles, and it was her debts at that time that worried her so, though, of course, it wasn't fit telling to a child. And they've gone on increasing ever since, till I'm sure I don't know how the mistress will go back to London, unless she finds some way out of 'em first.'

'And I must have been an extra expense to her,' said Fenella, with a sigh.

'Well, miss, you have — there's no denying it! what with your long illness, and your dresses, and hire of carriages, and all that. But the mistress did it with an object. So she's naturally disappointed at your refusing to marry Sir Gilbert. And to be "my lady" too, miss! I wonder how you can!'

'Mamma has hardly spoken to me for three days,' said Fenella.

'No, my dear! but she will, directly she sees you have changed your mind. She's had a many troubles in this life, poor dear lady! and it seems hard that you should add to 'em—don't it, now?'

'If you will do up my hair, I will go and speak to her about it,' said Fenella wearily; and half-an-hour later she walked into her mother's room.

'Mamma, I have come to tell you that I have made up my mind to accept Sir Gilbert's offer,' she said; 'but it must be on one condition, that you tell him my whole history. Tell it him without reserve, mamma; don't spare me in any way; and if, after hearing it, he should still wish to make me his wife, I will marry him!'

Mrs Barrington was just about to call her by her favourite name of a fool, and say she might as well have kept her wonderful condescension to herself, when it suddenly struck her that she might find a way by which to keep the game in her own hands. So she smiled sweetly instead, and answered.

'Well, Fenella, if this is the only condition on which you will listen to Sir Gilbert's suit, of course I must comply with it, but I have already told you my opinion of the matter. It is quixotic and unnecessary! and if he *does* propose to you afterwards (which I doubt), you must be doubly grateful to him in return. He has been waiting nearly a week for his answer, and I received a note from him this morning on the subject. I shall therefore write and tell him to call upon me this evening. Madame de Beaupré can chaperon you to the Thellussons. It is better that you should be out of the way, as the interview is likely to be a painful one.'

'I have been thinking a great deal about it,' replied Fenella, 'and I am sure it is the only right and honourable course to pursue. And if it fails, mamma (as doubtless it will), then you must let me go out as a governess or a companion, and earn my own living. It is unfair that I should be a burden on you any longer, just because I have been so wicked and so weak.'

'A governess!' thought Mrs Barrington as her daughter left the room. 'As if I could allow such a scandal, and with that face too! But if my right hand has not lost its cunning, I will contrive this marriage for her.'

When Sir Gilbert Conroy walked into her little *salon* that evening, he found her looking the very soul of honour and the pink of propriety, arrayed in a grey cashmere dress, with a white lace *fichu* that gave her almost the look of a quaker.

'No, no! Sir Gilbert,' she said playfully, as she saw his glance wander round the room, 'you will not find my little girl hidden under any of the sofa or chair covers. Fenella is spending the evening at the Thellussons. I thought it best she should be out of the way whilst you and I discuss this subject together.'

'I am afraid Miss Barrington's absence does not augur a favourable answer to my suit,' replied Sir Gilbert, flushing up to the roots of his fair hair.

'Indeed! you are quite mistaken! My daughter is exceedingly well disposed— shall I say *too* well disposed?—to receive your advances, and thinks highly of the compliment you pay her. But Fenella feels that you are the soul of honour, Sir Gilbert (as she is herself), and, therefore, before granting you an interview, she has set me a little task which she thinks I can execute better than she can.'

'A task!' echoed Sir Gilbert.

'Yes! I am sure you will laugh at us for a couple of silly women, and I told my daughter so; still, I could not blame her decision, as it was founded on the very principles it has been the aim and object of my life to instil into her.'

'You alarm me, Mrs Barrington! Pray don't keep me in suspense,' gasped the baronet.

'Indeed, I will not, for it is not worth while,' laughed the lady pleasantly. 'The fact is, Sir Gilbert, about a year ago my silly child had one of those foolish love affairs which we all know of, and laugh at, —a boy - and - girl flirtation, which never could have come to anything, and which she had almost forgotten, until the agitation caused by your very flattering proposal recalled it to her mind. And then she begged me to tell you of it before you met again. I thought it perfectly unnecessary to worry you about such a trifle, and told her so; but Fenella's soul is of so pure and lofty a character that I cannot bear to dull even its lightest aspiration. She is so truthful, so honourable, so open, Sir Gilbert. Her mind is like a sheet of crystal.'

'Yes,' stammered the baronet uneasily; 'but — but — about this love affair, Mrs Barrington? Are you quite certain she *has* forgotten all about it, or that it may not crop up to disturb our domestic felicity? Is the gentleman in England still? Is she likely to meet him again?'

Mrs Barrington was annoyed that he took her communication so seriously.

'In England? Oh, dear, no! He went to the colonies, or he's dead—or something. I forget which. But he was such a boy, it's really not worth inquiring. And as for Fenella meeting him again — why, my dear Sir Gilbert, she wouldn't speak to him if she saw him in the streets to-morrow!'

'But these first attachments are sometimes the most enduring, you know, Mrs

Barrington ; and if your daughter had quite forgotten all about hers, I hardly think she would have considered it necessary to ask you to break the intelligence to me.'

Then Mrs Barrington could have bitten out her tongue that she had told him anything at all. It would have been just as easy to have assured Fenella that she had. She played with her fan, and looked virtuously reproachful.

' If you take it in that light, Sir Gilbert, I shall be indeed sorry that I spoke. *Need* I have said anything to you on the subject at all? It was only the extreme purity of my child's mind — the truthfulness of her feelings — that made her think of making such a confession! She would not go to you with even the shadow of a secret (however innocent) upon her soul. But it is only a mind of equal candour with her own that could appreciate the delicacy of her motives.'

' But I can — I do!' exclaimed Sir

Gilbert. ' I confess that one of the great
attractions that drew me to your daughter,
Mrs Barrington, was her youth and apparent innocence. I have grown sick and
weary of the women of the world, with
their artifice and falsehood and intrigues.
I long to have an unsophisticated, guile-
less maiden for my wife. Indeed, I would
put none else in the place once occupied
by my honoured mother. I come of an
old and unblemished family ; and one of
our proudest boasts is that no one has
ever been able to point the finger of scorn
at a Lady Conroy ! '

Mrs Barrington went pale with agitation.

' Good heavens ! Sir Gilbert, what are
you thinking of ? Would you link such
an expression as that with the silly little
flirtation I have just been foolish enough
to tell you of ? '

' No—certainly not,' he answered ; ' and
if I cannot secure even your lovely and
innocent daughter for my wife without

hearing that she has already been courted by one of my own sex, it is hopeless for me to look farther.'

'Unless you go to the nursery for your Lady Conroy,' laughed Mrs Barrington. 'But, unfortunately, I have no more daughters there, Sir Gilbert, or I should certainly ask you to go and take your choice of them. You are a son-in-law of whom any woman might be proud.'

'You are very good to say so, my dear madam,' replied the baronet. 'Am I to understand, then, that Miss Barrington consents to receive my offer for her hand ?'

'The silly creature waits to see if you will renew it after having heard this terrible secret of her former life—that she actually flirted for the space of a few weeks with a lad, who ought to have been whipped by his tutor for his precocity.'

'Miss Barrington might have been sure I should not have permitted such a trifle

to stand in the way of my happiness,' rejoined Sir Gilbert. 'At the same time, as
I confess I am rather sensitive on such
matters, will you ask her, as a personal
favour, not to allude to the subject before
me ? Perhaps it is as well I should have
heard it ; but having heard it, I should
wish to forget it again. Cannot it be
buried in oblivion ? I should like to try
and fancy (even if it be only a fancy) that
my wife never had a lover before myself.'

'And neither has she, my dear Sir Gilbert. You surely would not dignify the
wretched boy I spoke of by the name of
" lover "? However, I shall repeat your
wishes to Fenella, and I am certain they
will be attended to. When may I count
on the pleasure of seeing you again ?'

'With your permission I will call to-
morrow afternoon,' he said, as he rose
to take his leave. 'I shall not be quite
happy until I have learned Miss Barrington's decision from her own lips.'

'Well, of all the glaring pieces of

folly I ever took part in, this is the worst,' thought Mrs Barrington, when the baronet had disappeared. 'Fenella as nearly lost her chance of becoming Lady Conroy as possible, and entirely through her own fault. The idea of rousing a man's suspicions unnecessarily! I wish I had followed my own judgment and told him nothing. However, the girl is so strange, she might allude in some way to the matter, so it is as well, perhaps, that he should be prepared. But it must go no farther. I must impress on Fenella the absolute necessity of holding her tongue henceforward.'

As soon as she returned home from the Thellussons, Fenella ran up to her mother's room, eager to learn her fate.

'Well, mamma!' she exclaimed breathlessly, as she entered it, 'has he been?'

'Yes, certainly; Sir Gilbert is too much of a gentleman not to keep his appointments.'

'And you told him ?'

'I did !'

'*Everything?*'

'Everything !'

The girl leaned back against the wall, almost speechless from excitement.

'Oh!' she gasped. 'What *did* he say?'

'He said all that was most kind and courteous. His affection for you is great enough to surmount any obstacle. He renews his offer of marriage to you.'

The faint colour died out of Fenella's cheeks. It was evident which way her hopes had lain. But surprise was her predominant feeling at the news.

'You told Sir Gilbert *everything*, and yet he said that?' she asked incredulously.

'Haven't I answered the question already! Do you doubt my word?' returned Mrs Barrington, in a sharp voice.

'Oh no, mamma ; but it seems so wonderful to me! I thought when he heard it he would just walk out of the house and never come back again. What did you tell him? Does he know that I cannot pretend to love him; that—that— I cannot forget what is past, whatever pleasures the future may hold for me? I will be a good wife to him, mamma (as far as I can), and I shall always feel grateful for his forbearance in this matter; but I *hope* you told him that he must not expect any more?'

'If you will sit down and talk like a reasonable creature, instead of a woman out of a play, I will repeat exactly what passed between us,' replied Mrs Barrington.

She saw that it would be useless to try half measures with Fenella; that if her conscience were not entirely satisfied, she would probably speak to Sir Gilbert herself on the subject; and that, whilst she was about it, she might as well tell a good lie as a feeble one.

The girl sat down, but impatiently, with large wondering eyes of expectation still turned upon her mother.

'I told Sir Gilbert Conroy *everything*, from the beginning to the end,' commenced Mrs Barrington emphatically, whilst her daughter's face grew scarlet. 'Of course he was very much distressed at hearing it (who wouldn't be?); I am not sure that he didn't shed tears, but men are sensitive about such things, and he turned his head the other way.'

'How *good* of him,' murmured Fenella.

'He felt it *deeply*, there is no doubt— and so did I. It was anything but a pleasant task you set me, Fenella; but when his emotion had subsided, he told me it could make no difference in his affection for you; on the contrary (if anything), he loved you more for what you had suffered, and he repeated his offer to make you his wife.'

'He must be a very generous man,' said her daughter meditatively.

'He is more than generous,' replied Mrs Barrington; 'he is noble, chivalrous, heroic! But he coupled his decision with a request which I was obliged to accord him in your name, Fenella, and which you must be good enough to pay particular attention to.'

'What is it, mamma?' said the girl dreamily.

'Sir Gilbert said to me, " I am willing to overlook and forget all that is past, Mrs Barrington, on one condition, and that is, that a total silence is preserved on the subject henceforward. I love your daughter dearly, and am most desirous of making her Lady Conroy; but I am a proud man, and do not care to think that any one ever courted my wife before myself. I should wish to fancy (even if it be only fancy) that I am her first lover."'

'He can never be my *lover*,' cried Fenella quickly.

'Oh, don't be so tiresome,' said her

mother, 'catching one up in that rude way. It is not at all likely he *will* be your lover — husbands never are — but the thing is, that you are not to speak of, nor allude to the other; nor to anything, in fact, that happened before your marriage.'

'Am I likely to do so?' sighed Fenella, with her hand pressed upon her aching heart.

'Well, that's the condition, my dear, and I hope you understand it. Sir Gilbert is coming here to-morrow afternoon to receive his answer from your own lips. Just give it simply and say no more about it. Let the past be buried in oblivion, as he wishes it to be, and depend upon it you will be as happy a woman as the world contains. It is an excellent marriage, and I must say, after your *escapade* of last year, that you are a very lucky girl to secure it, and it is much more than you deserve.'

'I know that,' said Fenella, 'and I shall always be very grateful to Sir Gilbert for his kindness to me ; but as for being *happy*, mother, that is impossible.'

'Stuff and nonsense, child! Don't begin to *pose* for a martyr, and fancy you are being dragged into a marriage against your will, like the heroine of a novel.'

'Oh no! I should never be so silly as that, because I really wish to be married. I am sure I shall be happier with Sir Gilbert than I am at home,' replied the girl ingenuously.

'Well, I must say that's grateful of you ; and after all the trouble you've given me!' cried Mrs Barrington.

'Yes, I suppose I must have been the cause of a great deal of trouble and disappointment to you, mamma, and I am sorry for it ; but still, you know, we have not been very happy together, and if Sir Gilbert really loves me, I am sure I shall grow fond of him. My heart does *ache*

so for love sometimes,' cried Fenella, in a
voice of pain.

Mrs Barrington thought it just as well
to keep down her rising wrath, and be
polite to the future Lady Conroy.

'Well, my sweet girl, I acknowledge we
might have spent a pleasanter year than
the last ; but there have been *causes*, you
know, Fenella, and my maternal pride has
been sorely wounded. But it will be
better now, dearest, will it not ? Bennett
and I will do our utmost to get together
a decent trousseau for you, and once
launched on the world as Lady Conroy,
you will never remember your former
life except as an ugly dream.'

'Will he want it to be *soon* ?' faltered
Fenella.

'I should think so, my dear. Sir Gilbert is not a boy, you see, and there is
no reason for delay. I shall see you presented at Court before you are eighteen.'

'Yes, I was only seventeen last birth-
day,' said Fenella, with a piteous smile,

as the mention seemed to recall how much she had passed through before that time.

' Most people would take you for older,' remarked Mrs Barrington. ' Sir Gilbert thought you were nineteen or twenty.'

' The last year has made a woman of me ; I shall never be a girl again,' said her daughter, as she gathered up her evening wraps and retired to bed.

But the night did not bring much rest to her. Emphatically as Mrs Barrington had asserted that Sir Gilbert Conroy had been made acquainted with all the facts of her former life, Fenella was not satisfied. She had learnt to distrust her mother's statements—to discredit her pretty oaths and smiles, as she did her blooming cheeks and perfumed skin—and she lay awake, wondering how she could arrive at the truth for herself. She did not feel any particular agitation at the idea of seeing Sir Gilbert Conroy and telling him that she would be his wife.

Her heart was empty and sodden, and she thought she would just as soon marry him as remain single : it was all the same to her ; she could never feel very happy or very miserable again, and she believed that her future life would be more bearable passed with Sir Gilbert than with her mother. So that when the baronet entered her presence the following afternoon, he could detect nothing different from her usual appearance, except a questioning look in her eye, as if she longed to find out exactly what he thought of her. But she coloured when he approached her side, and he interpreted the action according to his own wishes.

'Miss Barrington,' he commenced, as he took her hand, 'your mother has, of course, prepared you for this interview. Am I right in conjecturing that you would not have granted it unless you intended to give me a favourable answer ?'

'Yes,' she said quietly, 'mamma has

told me all about it, and—I thank you, Sir Gilbert.'

' Does that mean that you will be my wife, Fenella ? '

' Since you wish it to be so—yes.'

At this answer Sir Gilbert naturally professed to be enraptured. He kissed the hand he held, and, not being rebuked for forwardness, kissed the fair face that glowed above it, and then he put his arm round her waist, and drew Fenella to a sofa, and sat down beside her, and talked of his mansion in town and his castle in Scotland—of the family jewels which had not been worn since the death of his mother, Lady Valeria Conroy, and how she had been the daughter of the Duke of Ben Nevis, whose kinsman, David of Ben Nevis, had fought side by side on the field of Bosworth with his own great ancestor, Gilbert de Conn, one of the ' roys' or ' kings' of Scotland. For Sir Gilbert's favourite hobby was the age and stainlessness of his family tree, and

he looked down with the supremest contempt on all the unfortunate ones of the
earth who could not produce a parchment
roll inscribed with their pedigree.

Fenella's parents were not noble, but
he had taken good care to ascertain before proposing to her that the family on
both sides was irreproachable. He would
not have transformed Venus Aphrodite
herself into Lady Conroy unless she had
been able to prove that she had respectable ancestors. But even the enumera-
tion and description of the late Lady
Valeria's diamonds and emeralds did not
seem to awaken much interest in the
bosom of the girl, who kept her clear,
grey eyes fixed upon Sir Gilbert with
the same questioning look in them with
which she had welcomed him.

' But,' she said presently, interrupting
him in the midst of a description of the
gardens at Conroy Castle, 'are you *quite*
sure that I shall be able to please you in
all things ? I am not a very loving girl,

you know (mamma will have told you that), and perhaps you might expect more from me than I shall feel myself able to perform.'

' I shall always do my utmost to meet your wishes, Fenella, and I hope you will be as ready to meet mine. I expect no more from you than that. Is it too much ? '

' Oh no ! How could I give you less ? ' she murmured. ' It is very, *very* good of you to accept so little,' and then, with a sudden impulse, she laid her hand upon his arm. ' Sir Gilbert, mamma said I was not to mention the subject, but I must—only this once. She told you last night everything — about — about — last year, and still you come and ask me to be your wife ! How can I ever be grateful enough to you for your forbearance to me ? '

He almost laughed at the varying colour which came and went in her cheeks, and made her look so earnest and so beautiful as she said the words.

'My dearest girl,' he answered, as he drew her closer to himself, 'I had already forgotten all about it. I am a man of the world, you see, Fenella, and used to hear all sorts of things; and although I confess that, just at first, I was a little disappointed, the unworthy feeling soon wore off again, and I am perfectly contented to take you *as you are!* Only—will you grant me one favour?—not to make the past a subject of constant allusion! Let it die out, my dear Fenella, and forget it yourself, as I have.'

'I will try,' she replied, in a low voice; and Sir Gilbert recommenced his description of the glories upon which she was about to enter, whilst she mused to herself in silence, and thought what a generous, noble heart he must have, and how good and grateful she should be in return.

Before he left in the evening, the weding was fixed for that day month. The baronet's only near relation was a married sister, who would be charmed to find an excuse to visit Paris, and so he thought the marriage had better take place at the English Embassy, with as little fuss as needful.

'Too soon! too soon! too terribly soon!' cried Mrs Barrington playfully. 'Why, my poor child will only be seventeen years and three months old! She oughtn't to *think* of marriage even for the next five years — ought you, Fenella, darling? However, I suppose you wilful lovers will have your own way!'

But a look from her daughter's eyes stopped Mrs Barrington's banter. She was still very much afraid of Fenella, and would feel relieved when those honest, serious eyes of hers were well out of the way.'

'Will the time we have fixed upon be agreeable to you?' said Sir Gilbert, turning to Fenella.

The girl started and flushed.

'Oh yes; it is all the same to me! That is—I mean—I would rather please

you than myself. It is the least I can
do in return for all your goodness to
me.'

That was the keynote of her life thence-
forward, and her belief in it made her
marriage seem almost a gladsome thing.
She grew more and more contented with
her prospects as the days went on. She
felt that, by God's mercy, she was going to
lead an honourable and useful life for the
future, and she tried to persuade herself
that she was happy.

But there were times—sad times alone
and in the dark—when the picture was re-
versed, and the past came back so vividly
upon her memory that she was ready to
leap out of bed, and write to Sir Gilbert
and say she had been mad, and that never
—never—never could she be his wife—
nor the wife of any man. Times—when
the passionate looks and tones of Geoffrey
Doyne, as she remembered them upon the
sands of Ines-cedwyn, would return to
torture her with their dead sweetness—

when she fancied she could hear his voice, and see his eyes, and feel the very clasp of his arms about her beating heart. And the present and the future would become a black and mighty void, and she stood face to face with the living, unforgotten past. But Fenella had strength at least to battle with such memories, and call herself hard names for weeping over them. She would resolutely stamp upon the vision ; she would pray until she had drowned the voice ; she would tell herself that she was worse than a fool even to bestow another thought upon the man who had been so base as to betray her. He was a traitor, she would say to herself, with the tears streaming down her face—a traitor and a liar ! He *must* be, else why did he swear to keep to her alone when he knew he was going to marry another woman ? Why did he accept her vows of fidelity when he was about to break his own ? She would be brave—she would be strong—she would tear his very image from her heart; she would not shelter there one who could be so cowardly and so untrue to her and to himself.

Ah, how many women have said the same before! How many tortured wretches have cried to God to take away the memory that rose before them like a mocking devil, gibing at their despair! And with all their resolutions, their oaths, and their prayers, how hard it is—how bitterly hard—to erase a true love (however unworthy) from the heart! The man who is bound by swathes too powerful for him to rend asunder, may be strong, and courageous, and determined. He may fight like a lion for his release, he may strain every nerve and muscle to get free; but if the bonds are beyond his physical capability to rupture, he will only injure himself, and sink back again, exhausted by his efforts. It were wiser for him to accept the inevitable, and get up and walk through the world with as much case as his crippled condition will allow him.

So Fenella waked up at the appointed time, to find that she was the wife of Sir Gilbert Conroy ; waited on with all attention and kindness by her husband, and surrounded by every luxury that money could procure for her.

Yet the swathes were around her still, and she would lie bound with them in her coffin.

CHAPTER VI.

SMOOTH WATERS.

'It is vain that we would coldly gaze
  On such as smile upon us : the heart must
  Leap kindly back to kindness.'—*Byron.*

WHETHER from intuition, or the common-sense that charac-terised most of his actions, Sir Gilbert Conroy went just the right way to win such kindly feeling as it was in the power of his young wife to bestow upon him. He treated her as a friend. He did not (after the usual manner of bride-grooms) load her with caresses and com-pliments until she was sick of flattery. Neither did he sit gazing at her hour after hour, as if he could not satisfy himself with

the contemplation of her beauty. Had he
done so, Fenella would probably have
become shy and distant with him, or
openly expressed her dislike to his behaviour, and then quarrels would have
ensued between them. But there was
nothing in Sir Gilbert's attentions from
which the most delicate nature could have
revolted ; he was chivalry itself. He
waited on his wife in public with the
greatest assiduity, anticipating every wish,
and never permitting her to do a single
thing for herself. Still, he would have
done as much for any lady confided to his
charge.

Even in private, although he was always
polite and affectionate in his manner towards her, he was never exacting. He
allowed her to follow her inclinations in
the matter of their intercourse, rather than
to press his own upon her. So that after
a few days Fenella lost her shyness, and
became quite friendly and intimate with
her husband, and after a few weeks she

would have missed him very much had he been called away from her.

The fact is, Sir Gilbert Conroy was not in love with Fenella, and never had been. Her chief attraction in his eyes (as he had told her mother) was her youth and innocence. He was weary of the fickleness and falsehood of fashionable women (as, indeed, he had just cause to be), and he believed that Fenella would make a Lady Conroy of whom he need never be ashamed. Of course he admired her. He was not quite such a stoic at five-and-thirty as to have lost all faith in female beauty, but he had seen handsomer women—as he coolly informed his sister, Lady Marjoram, on the day of the wedding. And Lady Marjoram, who was one of the most charming women who ever spent her life in a round of frivolity, had shaken her head at him and said,—

‘You’re as bad as ever, Bertie. I believe you’d pick holes in the Venus de

Milo if she could find those lost arms of
hers and wind them round you. But
mark my words—Fenella may not be as
beautiful as some of your former loves, but
she is a better woman than the whole lot
of them put together. She's the first girl
that has ever taken your fancy who is fit
to fill our mother's place.'

'I believe you there,' replied Sir Gilbert.

'And I hope you'll be a good boy
to her, Bertie, and put the thought of
that horrid Mrs Messiter out of your
head altogether,' continued his sister more
seriously.

'You may be sure of that, Janie,' was
his quick reply. 'That portion of my life
is over for ever.'

And Sir Gilbert was right. That portion of his life during which he had been
held in thrall by an unprincipled woman,
who cared for nothing but using his purse
and gratifying her own vanity, was over
for ever. It had extended over many

years, and been the cause of much anxiety
to his family, who feared it might stand
in the way of his settlement; but it
was done with, and it would never be
renewed.

Sir Gilbert was too honourable a man
to deceive the girl whom he had made his
wife. He would exact the utmost propriety of conduct from Lady Conroy, and
he would render her the same in return.
But an old attachment is not to be forgotten in a day, and the remembrance of
Mrs Messiter tended to make the baronet
more deferential in his manners towards
Fenella than he would otherwise have
been. And she was so glad of it. She
was so thankful that he did not call her
'darling,' and make her sit upon his lap,
and try and force confessions of love from
her, which she would have been unable to
refuse to make without offending him. It
was so much nicer as it was (she said to
herself); and she actually began to feel a
sort of affection for Sir Gilbert, because he

did not exhibit it too freely towards her.
The life they led together was like a dream
of fairyland to the girl, who had left a convent school only to see Ines-cedwyn and
Sainte Pauvrette.

Sir Gilbert took her for a month to Italy,
previous to their returning to London for
the season ; and as the days went on,
Fenella began to ask herself if she were
asleep or awake, everything was so new
and wonderful to her ; she had not believed
that living could be made so easy.   If she
wished to dress for the evening or for
walking, her robes were laid in readiness
for her, and her new maid was in obse-
quious attendance, ready to put them on ;
if she rose to leave the room or the house,
a man-servant sprang up to open the door,
to carry her shawl, or to receive the orders
she might wish to leave behind her.   She
was never permitted to walk, especially
through the streets ; a carriage was always
at her beck and call ; and her purse was
liberally supplied with money to make any

purchase she might feel inclined for. Her
husband considered that it was his duty to
see that Fenella preserved a certain amount
of state—not for her own sake, but for
that of Lady Conroy—and he would have
done the same for the honour of the name
she bore, had his wife been the ugliest old
woman in Christendom. But the girl did
not consider this. Her path was strewn
with roses for her ; her husband was always
kind and courteous ; and her heart was a
grateful one, and responded accordingly.
Even when they returned to their town
house in Portman Square, the pleasure
continued. The first coming back to London was painful to her—she could not
deny that—but she shook the feeling off
bravely, and her new sister-in-law soon
made her feel at home.

It has already been said that Lady Marjoram was a very sweet woman. She was,
moreover, a very grand lady (as titles go),
and her family were proud of the connec-
tion, but no accession to rank and fortune

had been able to spoil her unaffected
womanly nature.

Her husband was Henry Frederick
Charles Albert Ernest, fifth Earl of
Marjoram and tenth Baron Carberry,
with an annual rent-roll of twenty thousand, and estates in all the countries of the
United Kingdom. He was a fat, good-
tempered, farmerlike - looking person of
middle age, who allowed his countess to
have her own way in everything, and
expected to enjoy the same privileges
himself.

This very grand sister-in-law might,
under ordinary circumstances, have turned
up her nose at her brother's choice, and
would, under *most* circumstances (for some
of the worst-bred women in the world
are to be found sheltering their vulgarity
beneath the strawberry leaves), have mixed
up so much condescension in her intercourse with the young and portionless
girl as to turn her politeness into an
insult. But Lady Marjoram was a gentle-

woman, and that is a rank which, if we do not inherit it from the goodness of our own hearts, no strawberry leaves can give us. She had been working 'like a nigger' (as she herself expressed it) to get the Portman Square house into proper order for the Conroys' first season in town ; and as soon as Fenella was ensconced in it, Lady Marjoram flew to her side, and offered her every assistance in her power.

'Of course you must be presented at Court, dear,' she said,—'that must be the first thing ; and then you must give dinners and receptions, and all kinds of horrors! Oh, how I hated them when I married Marjoram ; but they must be done, you know. And if you wish it, I'll come and help you through with everything that your cook and housekeeper can't do for you.'

The kind tone and feeling of her sister-in-law moved Fenella deeply. She pressed closer to Lady Majoram and thanked her, with the tears in her eyes.

'Why, my dear child, what is this?' cried the Countess; 'you didn't suppose I was going to leave you to do it all by yourself, did you? I am not quite such a wretch as that comes to. I remember too well what I suffered when I married Marjoram, and the old Countess-Dowager wouldn't give me a single hint, and only found fault with everything I did. But is the house as you like it, Fenella? Can you suggest any alteration?'

'Nothing, dear Lady Marjoram; it is just perfect, I assure you.'

'You mustn't call me Lady Marjoram. I must be Janie to you, Fenella. Don't forget that we are sisters, though I suppose I am nearly old enough to be your mother. What is your age, dear?'

'I was seventeen last January,' replied Fenella, with a little sigh.

'And how do you and my brother get on together? Does he treat you kindly? Are you quite happy with him?'

Fenella opened her eyes.

'Oh, Janie! what a question. Of course he is kind to me—very, very kind.'

'No "*of course*" in the matter, my dear. The generality of men are brutes, and marriage (as a rule) is a mistake. Not but what my Marjoram is an awfully good old fellow; I wouldn't change him for the world. And my brother is a gentleman, too, which is, after all, the main thing. A woman can generally get on with a gentleman, whether she loves him or not; but so very few men *are* gentlemen to their wives! It's a lost art, Fenella. The man who would fell another to the ground for daring to say he was *not* a gentleman, will behave in the rudest manner to the unfortunate woman who is compelled to listen to whatever he may choose to say to her.'

'I am not an unfortunate woman,' laughed Fenella softly; 'Gilbert has never said a rude word to me.'

'I'm very glad to hear it, my dear; and I think I know my brother well enough to say that he never will. You will find Gilbert very particular—in fact, he's a bit of a prude ; but so long as you remain what you are now — innocent, modest, and refined in your speech and manners—he will make you the best of husbands. Gilbert couldn't stand a woman that was talked of. He is very fond of you and very proud of you, and so he ought to be ; but he is fonder and prouder of his family name (that has been his weakness from a boy), and I believe he would kill the woman he loved, with his own hand, sooner than she should disgrace it.'

' I will never disgrace it,' said Fenella, in a low voice.

' I am sure you won't,' rejoined Lady Marjoram heartily, as she took the girl in her arms and affectionately embraced her.

Under the tuition and guidance of her sister-in-law, all those ordeals which appear so terrible to a young wife, first launched upon the fashionable world, were transformed into pleasures; and Fenella had been presented at Court, and attended her first ball, and given her first dinner-party before she had time to wonder whether she should be a success or a failure.

The upshot was that she proved an undoubted success. Introduced everywhere by the Countess of Marjoram, the youthful Lady Conroy became an object of universal attention and admiration. The extreme delicacy of her skin, the clearness of her complexion, and the child-like hue of her soft fair hair, all combined to make Fenella look even younger than she was; and as it was one of Sir Gilbert's fancies that she should always appear dressed in white, she soon gained the name of 'The Lily' in the circles she frequented. The baronet mentioned this fact to his sister, with pride beaming in his eyes.

'I don't approve,' he said, 'of the

modern custom of giving nicknames to ladies of rank; but since the licence has unfortunately been allowed to creep into society, they could not have chosen one for Lady Conroy that would have offended me less.'

'That would have pleased you more, you mean,' cried Lady Marjoram, laughing. 'Take care, Sir Gilbert de Conn— Roy of Scotland! If you don't mind your P's and Q's, you'll be guilty of the plebeian crime of falling in love with your own wife.'

The baronet took her jest quite seriously.

'No, Janie; I assure you I feel nothing of that kind for Fenella, and neither does she for me. We are the best of friends, and nothing more. That is as it should be. Any warmer feeling than friendship is sure to suffer from so close a contact. By the way, she asked me yesterday if she might take singing lessons. What shall I do about it?'

'Get her the very best master you can,' replied his sister decidedly. 'Let her have Signor Possetrina. She has a lovely voice, and is fond of music. Besides, she is the very best little girl in the world, and you must give her every mortal thing she has a fancy for.'

'You are quite right,' said Sir Gilbert, 'and I will engage Signor Possetrina for her at once.'

These singing lessons soon became Fenella's greatest pleasure, and, under the tuition of the best master in town, she made rapid progress. Signor Possetrina was charmed both with her voice and her ability. He found her well grounded in the art, and he was never tired of praising the purity of her tones, the delicacy of her ear, and the earnestness with which she pursued her studies. She would have given up her engagements for her music, if Sir Gilbert would have permitted such a sacrifice to art. But every spare hour she spent at her piano, and her singing soon began to be talked of as much as her face had been.

'Almost too much talked of,' as Sir Gilbert remarked, with a shrug of his shoulders, to Lady Marjoram. 'I hope she's not going to turn out a genius, Janie. Geniuses are generally erratic sort of persons, with wills of their own, and I shouldn't care for Lady Conroy to become too decided and clever.'

'Bertie, you're a fool,' rejoined his sister (it is only sisters that can call men 'fools' with impunity; they won't stand it from their wives); 'wouldn't you rather your children had a clever mother than a stupid one? Besides, do you imagine women are any the less obstinate or deceitful for being boobies? Not a bit of it! It's the wives that have no intellectual qualities wherewith to amuse themselves, that try and get their amusement out of flirting, and sometimes even out of champagne.'

'*Don't*, Janie,' said Sir Gilbert, with a shudder.

'Well, then, my dear boy, be sensible, and let Fenella sing all day, and all night too, if she wishes it, so long as she is contented with no more dangerous audience than old Signor Possetrina and yourself.'

So Fenella was allowed to follow her talent to her heart's content, and it did content her wonderfully. Her music sang to her—sadly enough, and yet sweetly—of her unforgotten past. Geoffrey's tones (although unconsciously to herself) were wafted back from the shores of memory, upon the wings of song; and whilst Fenella sat at the piano, she would wander off into the realms of fancy, picturing a future perhaps in which all the crooked paths of this world would be made straight, and all the rough places plain, and lose herself in impossible dreams, until she was recalled to earth again, and found her cheeks were wet with tears.

Yet she was happy; as happy as any one can be who has outlived the thoughtlessness of childhood—because it is impossible to grow up and think, without weeping for ourselves or others. There were times, indeed, when a chance word or look—a chord of music, or the scent of a flower—would bring back the remembrance of Geoffrey Doyne so powerfully on Fenella's mind, as to make her sick with longing to see his face once more (if only for a moment). But it was the sort of feeling with which we regard the dead—those hallowed dead whose still, white features we sometimes feel as if we would give our lives to look on once again. It had no more hope, and no more real desire of being realised, than we have of unsoldering the coffins that have been closed so long.

There was one trait in Fenella's character which somewhat puzzled Lady Marjoram; she seemed to think so tenderly of little children, and yet to be almost ashamed if detected in any kindness towards them. The Countess had a nursery full of little ones, from big boys and girls of twelve and fourteen, to a tiny stranger who had only made his appearance in this wicked world about three months previously. Lady Marjoram thought very little of babies; they were amongst the natural nuisances of this life, she said, that must be endured. She romped with all her children alike, from the eldest to the youngest, and was quite offended if one of them dared to be weakly or sick. It was unlike either herself or Marjoram, she would declare; and if the brat didn't get well soon, she should begin to think that he had been changed at nurse.

'Take the boy! he won't break,' she exclaimed one day, as she threw her infant into Fenella's arms.

Something—what was it?—swelled in the girl's breast as she received the little creature, and the tears rushed suddenly to her eyes.

'Please take him back again,' she faltered to her sister-in-law; 'I—I—am not much used to babies.'

'You mean you don't like them, my dear.   Well, I don't wonder at it.   Nobody does until they have them of their own.   But you must get your hand in, you know, Lady Conroy.   Bertie won't be satisfied till he has a son.'

'No, I suppose not,' replied Fenella, 'and some day I hope he may have one.'

'How quietly you said that, child! too quietly a great deal for your age.   One would think you had had a dozen.'

Fenella coloured.

'I *am* older than my age, Janie,' she said, with a sigh; 'but I was not always so happy as I am now.'

'I expect not,' thought Lady Marjoram; and then she asked, as a natural sequence,

' Have you heard lately of Mrs Barrington,
Fenella ? '

' I have not, and I feel rather anxious
about it. She was to have been in town
last month, and then she caught this attack
of low fever, and Bennett seems to think
it may be some time yet before she is
able to move. I am sure she must be
very weak, or she never would have
missed coming to town for the season.'

' Well, the season may be said to be
over now, so I suppose Mrs Barrington
will not join you until you go to Conroy
Castle.'

' I do not see how it will be possible,
Janie. Gilbert told me yesterday that
we must be there by the twelfth.'

' Of course, for the grouse ! Bertie
would not miss the first day of the
season for anything. Sport is his great
pastime, Fenella ; he loves it as enthu-
siastically as you do, music. You must
never throw any obstacle in the way of
his pursuing it.'

'Why should I ?' asked Fenella simply.

She was quite at her ease in the presence of her husband, but she was equally happy when he was absent. Her present content did not arise from being married to him (though she may have deceived herself into thinking so) ; it was due rather to the fact that he never urged the circumstance of their marriage too strongly on her notice. Her relations with her mother had caused Fenella some uneasiness since she had become Lady Conroy. Mrs Barrington had appeared to imagine that she ought to derive as many advantages from the marriage as her daughter, and Sir Gilbert had not seen the matter in the same light. Indeed, the greatest drawback in his eyes to marrying Fenella had been the existence of her mother. He despised the widow's character from every point of view—he would have removed his wife entirely from her influence had he been able, and the last thing he desired was that she should continue to exert it. Fenella had, therefore, been placed in a very difficult position,—forced to read and answer Mrs Barrington's letters of reproach, and complaints of poverty, on the one hand, and to bear with equanimity Sir Gilbert's animadversions on her mother's conduct, on the other.

At last the difference of opinion had been settled by the baronet giving his wife permission to invite Mrs Barrington to stay with them for a month, either in London or Scotland, but this invitation (as has already been shown) she was unable through illness to accept. Fenella could not feel quite sorry about it,—not so sorry as, she told herself, she ought to feel—because she had a premonition that Mrs Barrington's advent would not be productive of increased happiness in her married life. She would rather be with Gilbert alone, she thought. Her mother's presence could only remind her of the darkest passages in her young life.

And she was spared the ordeal she had
begun to dread ; for she and her husband
had only been settled in Scotland for a
fortnight, when the news reached them
from Paris that Mrs Barrington had succumbed to the weakness supervening her
attack of fever.

CHAPTER VII.

A REVELATION.

'Thy words have darted hope into my soul,
And comfort dawns upon me.'—*Southern.*

IT was naturally a great shock to Fenella's nervous system to hear of her mother's death. It is a shock to learn (thus unexpectedly) of the death of any one whom we have lately seen in apparent health and strength. And it seemed so impossible to picture Mrs Barrington dead, and laid out in her coffin. Mrs Barrington, with her painted cheeks and skin, her dyed hair, her toilettes of pink and blue and silver, her artificial ways and words and looks.

Fenella could not realise her mother shorn
of these frivolous accompaniments; she
wondered how she would get on without
them, even in the other world. But when
the first shock was over, the girl's honest
heart could not pretend there was much
grief remaining for their present separation. There might have been. Mrs Barrington, in repulsing her daughter's affection, had thrust from her a rich store
of love that might have been her con-
solation and her stay till her life's end.
But love is a plant of growth; it can
no more live without nourishment than
a flower can flourish without earth and
water. And Mrs Barrington had killed
the beautiful blossom that was springing
up in her child's heart. She had trampled
it under foot and neglected it, and it had
perished for lack of food. And now
that she had passed out of sight, she had
not left one loving memory in Fenella's
mind by which to mourn her. On the
contrary, her daughter, in deference to the

fact that she had been her father's wife, and she was dead, felt herself compelled, resolutely, to put away all thoughts of her, since remembrance brought reproach in its train.

But she could not help thinking of Bennett—dear good old Bennett, who had been with them before her own birth, and who had been so attached to her late mistress; she was terribly anxious to know what was to become of Bennett. The servant was no longer young—she was at least fifty years of age, twenty of which had been spent in their service; and she had become so wedded to their ways, it was unlikely she would find another place to suit her. Fenella wanted to send for her at once to Conroy Castle. There was a baby expected there in the spring, and her wish was to instal Eliza Bennett as head of the nursery.

'She loves me,' she said to her husband, with big pathetic eyes, 'and she will take every care of our little child for my sake.'

Sir Gilbert was good-naturedly disposed to acquiesce in anything his wife might desire. He was going over to Paris to attend the funeral of his mother-in-law, and, had the truth been known, in a more contented frame of mind than he would have cared to exhibit openly. Mrs Barrington had been his *bête noire*, but she was (fortunately) removed to a better sphere; it was quite immaterial to him what became of the servant.

'Do just as you like about it, my dear,' he replied. 'I have no doubt the old woman will be quite as efficient a guardian for the heir-apparent as anyone else.'

'Oh, Gilbert, you are so very good to me!' murmured Fenella gratefully. 'Then I will write Bennett a letter, dear, and you shall deliver it to her yourself.'

In consequence of which, Bennett, having first paid a short visit to her brother in Ines-cedwyn, arrived at Conroy Castle robed in the deepest mourning, and clasped

her young mistress in her arms again. Had
it been a meeting between a mother and
child it could hardly have been more
affectionate. The servant forgot all the
grandeur attendant on Sir Gilbert and
Lady Conroy, as she showered kiss after
kiss on Fenella's face; and the girl herself was scarcely less delighted to lay her
head on that kind, homely breast once
more.

There was a link between Bennett and
herself which nothing on this earth could
have the power to rupture. The servant
was, of course, full of the account of Mrs
Barrington's illness and death, and for
awhile neither of them could speak of anything else.

'And to think, dear Miss Fenella,' cried
Bennett, who could not get out of the
habit of using the old name, 'that you
shouldn't have been with us at the time!
But it was so sudden, my dear; the doctor
was as surprised as any of us—for we had
thought she was doing so nicely, poor dear

lady, and would be able to be moved at the
farthest in a week or two.   But she sank
(as you may say) in a few hours—nothing
would save her ; and her teeth was so fixed
we couldn't even get a drop of brandy and
water down her throat.'

'Did she speak of me, Bennett ? Did
she send me any message ?' demanded
Fenella timidly.

'Oh, she spoke often of you when she
was in the fever, my dear ; and she used to
talk of Conroy Castle, and the time when
she'd get here, and what a fine place it
was, and all that.   Poor dear ! little she
thought she'd never see it.   And as for
me, Miss Fenella, it seems as if my hands
was empty, now she's gone.   She was just
like a child to me—so sweet and amiable—
always wanting this or that.   It was " Bennett, come here !" or " Bennett, go there !"
all day long.   She didn't seem to be able
to do anything without her poor Bennett
—did she, now ?'

'No ; I am sure she looked on you as

her very best friend, Bennett, and I shall do the same for her sake. But when she was dying—when the end came—couldn't poor mamma speak then? Didn't she say one word of me, or send me any message?'

'Well, miss, you see, I don't think your poor dear mamma knew as her death was so near at hand, for she only seemed a little more fractious-like to me. I had just handed her some *limonade*, and I suppose she wanted *tisane*, bless her! for she pushed it aside and spilt it all over the counterpane, and said, "Take it away." And them was her last words, Miss Fenella; for as I was setting the bed to rights, I see a change come over her face, and I caught her up in my arms, and she was gone. I couldn't believe it. You might have knocked me over with a feather.' And Bennett buried her face in her rough hands, and cried like a little child. 'She was my life, Miss Fenella—just my life and nothing else,' she sobbed. 'It seemed as if I hadn't a will of my own when she was near—as if I couldn't move hand nor foot unless she ordered me. You know how I used to wait on her from morning till night. And now the world seems empty. I shall never have any rest for thinking of her. I wouldn't mind twice the trouble if I could only have her back again.'

Fenella tried to comfort the good-hearted creature with some of those ordinary arguments which sound like empty wind to ears on which a beloved voice has ceased to fall.

'You mustn't fret, dear Bennett. You must try and think how much better it is for her to be free of all the trouble of this world. I don't think poor mamma can have been very happy here. She always seemed full of worry and anxiety ; and now—now we must hope that it is all over, and—and—that she is in heaven,' said Fenella hesitatingly.

'In *heaven!* my dear lady!' replied Bennett, wiping her eyes. 'Yes, I'm sure of *that!* I know for certain as my darling mistress is walking in her robes of glory, with her 'arp in her 'and—and not a more beautiful angel in the whole place. Oh, yes! *she's* happy now, if *any one* is, miss. It isn't her (sweet angel!) as I'm thinking of—it's myself, and you, poor lamb! it's what *we* shall do without her.'

'We must try and comfort each other,' said Fenella gently. 'And now tell me of your brother, dear Bennett, and of Martha. Were you glad to see them again, and are they well and happy?'

Eliza Bennett coloured and looked ill at ease.

'Oh, yes! Miss Fenella—that is, my lady—Ben and Martha was looking well enough, and of course they was glad to see me, notwithstandin' the sad event as took me there.' And then she continued rather irrelevantly, 'I always carried out all your poor dear mamma's wishes to the very letter, Miss Fenella; there was never nothing she told me to do but what I thought it right to obey her; and I hope

it *has* been right, or if not, that the
Almighty won't lay it to my charge.   But
I made a sort of idol of her, Miss Fenella ; and I know that's wrong, and sometimes we're punished for doing of it—still,
when she *was* my mistress, I considered
myself bound to serve her, even to the
uttermost farthing.'

Fenella stared at this address — it
seemed so uncalled for ; but she answered warmly,—

' I am sure God, who looks on our
hearts, dear Bennett, will never blame
you for doing *more* than your duty.
The majority of us do so much less.
But I should like to hear something
about your own affairs.   Did poor mamma
pay you your wages ? I know they had
been due for a long time ; and has she
left any debts in Paris ? '

Bennett looked round cautiously, and
lowered her voice.

' Well, my dear, to my thinking, your
good gentleman must have cleared 'em off.

I know there *was* some, but after the
funeral he called me into the *salon*, and
paid me my wages, and something very
handsome over, and told me I was to
pack up my dear mistress's bits of jewellery for you, and to consider her wardrobe
as my own, which I thought was most
generous of him. And then I ventured
to ask him about the bills, and Sir Gilbert
said I wasn't to worry my head on the
matter, as he would see to 'em himself.'

'Dear Gilbert!' said Fenella. 'Oh!
he is so good and so generous to me,
nurse. I don't know what I have done
to deserve so kind a husband.'

'And such a fine-looking gentleman,
too, Miss Fenella; and such a princely
home! It does my heart good to see
you so comfortable and so happy. Ah!
if my poor dear mistress had only lived
to enjoy it with us!'

'Yes; I never thought that I *could* be
so happy,' said Fenella gravely.

'I've heard there's an old saying,

" *All's well as ends well*," my dear, and I am sure *you* ought to be able to understand it. But I see you wear that old locket still, Miss Fenella.'

Fenella coloured, and put her hand up to her bosom, in which reposed the present that Geoffrey Doyne had given her.

'Oh yes! I promised I would wear this till my death, nurse. Nothing can make any difference to that, you know.'

'And don't Sir Gilbert notice it, my dear?'

'He has never mentioned it to me, and I don't think he ever will. He is not that sort of man. He has a soul above such trifles.'

'Ah, well! you got a lucky exchange,' replied the servant; but her young mistress turned the conversation, and she said no more.

As the weeks went on, however, and the influence of the dead woman was farther and farther removed from her, Bennett became at one and the same time

more confidential and more reserved with
Lady Conroy. It seemed as though she
had some revelation at the very tip of her
tongue which she longed, and yet did not
dare to make. The temptation seemed
greatest when she was assisting Fenella
with the usual preparations for the expected heir ; and sometimes as together
they inspected and arranged the lace and
muslin and fine linen that arrived from
London to fill the nursery wardrobe,
Bennett seemed almost unable (as she
herself expressed it) to keep her tongue
between her teeth.

'Lor' bless us !' she exclaimed one
day, as she tossed some baby-linen almost impatiently to one side ; 'to think
of the pounds and pounds as is thrown
away just to decorate one infant, as you
may say, whilst another poor little creature
has hardly enough clothes to its back !
If *I* was a fine lady, like you, my dear,
with heaps of money to spend as I chose,
I should give a little thought to them as

has none, if I wanted my own child to thrive and do well.'

Fenella looked up at this tirade, surprised but smiling.

'Dear nurse,' she said, 'I believe we give a great deal away annually in charity as it is, but if there are any particular cases of want that you know of, I shall be only too glad to relieve them. I should like to do it (as you say) in hopes it might come back in a blessing on my own baby.'

The servant looked mollified.

'You was always good and sweet, my dear, from a little child. You take after your blessed mamma in heaven for that. I daresay a lot of money *does* go from this house to the poor—and food, and blankets, and what not beside; but if I was to ask you, Miss Fenella, for a few pounds for a little one as has got no mother and no father (so to speak)—for such a little one as we might both have heard of, you know, in our day—what

would you say then, my dear? Would
you give it?'

Fenella's trembling hands began to
play at once with the fastening of her
purse, from which she managed to extract a ten-pound note ; but before she
could hand it over to the servant, her
fortitude gave way, and sinking down on
her knees by the bedside, she burst into
a flood of tears.

Bennett left her place, and approaching
the spot where her mistress knelt, laid
her hand gently on the bowed head.

'So you haven't forgotten yet, my
lamb?' she whispered.

'*Forgotten!* My God! No; I shall
never, *never* forget!'

She knelt for a few minutes in the same
position, then rising suddenly, turned with
an April smile upon the servant.

'Am I not silly, nurse?—as great a
baby as when you brought me home from
the convent? But here's the note for
the little one you spoke of — and may

God bless it! And if there are any others that I can help in the same way, let me hear of them. I have more money, dear nurse, than I know how to spend; and I have less—less expenses than I might have had.'

The servant took the note and put it carefully away.

'Dear heart!' she thought, as Lady Conroy left the room. 'I'm sorely per-plext to know what's best to be done. It seems so hard she shouldn't know; and yet, now she's living so happy and loving and grand, 'twould be a pity to rake up old scores. Well, this isn't the time, any way. She's got too much on her mind just now to think of anything else. And perhaps I need never tell her; it looks likely enough.'

And, indeed, at that moment Fenella had what is technically termed 'her hands full.' The castle was filled with Christmas visitors, amongst which were the Earl and Countess of Marjoram, who had with them a cousin, Lord Laurence Grantham, a fine manly young fellow of five-and-twenty, who established himself from the very first as Fenella's chief friend and knight-errant. Lady Marjoram had not brought any of her children with her. She left home, she affirmed, to enjoy herself, and had no desire to keep her domestic miseries for ever in sight.

'You will be quite of my opinion in another year's time, my dear Fenella,' she said to her sister-in-law, 'and only too thankful to leave Portman Square or Conroy Castle, or wherever the nursery may be located, behind you. I positively begin to hate children, and believe they are only sent into this world to plague their parents out of it. Mine have had measles and hooping-cough already this year, and now they've all broken out with ringworm; so I couldn't stand it any longer, but packed the whole lot off to Bournemouth for the winter. There

they are, nine of them, with a governess
and two nurses, eating their heads off,
and sending us in weekly bills that make
Marjoram swear in the most awful manner. It's no use laughing, Fenella. You'll
laugh on the wrong side of your mouth
some day, my dear. Wait till you have
nine.'

'I hope I shall wait a long time,' rejoined Lady Conroy, who was much
amused at her sister-in-law's indignation.
'But what is it that Lord Marjoram is
speaking to Gilbert about?'

'About a vacant governorship at Sovooranooko, on the Gold Coast of Africa,
my dear, where yellow fever and smallpox
reign triumphantly from January to December, and elephants are shot for the sake
of their steaks, and alligators appear at the
breakfast-table *en papillotes* like sardines.'

'What interest can that have for Gilbert?' demanded Fenella, rather anxiously.
'He would never accept an appointment
in such a climate as that?'

'He says he should enjoy it above all things, Lady Conroy,' interposed Lord Laurence Grantham mischievously. 'He is already consulting Marjoram now about the proper - sized " bore " for elephant-shooting, and they are going down to the stackyard after luncheon to practise alligator-spearing.'

'Oh, the poor cows!' laughed the Countess. 'Marjoram will most likely get a spear in the calf of his leg, and be out of temper for the rest of the day!'

'Gilbert! you would never really go to a place like Sovooranooko?' said Fenella, as she went up to her husband's side.

'My dear child, what nonsense! what are you thinking of?' replied Sir Gilbert. 'I am about as likely to go to Timbuctoo!'

'Oh no, you are not!' retorted his sister. 'There are no elephants there.'

But his wife was quite satisfied with his answer, and troubled her head no further in the matter.

When February came round again with its pale spring flowers, a little daughter was born at Conroy Castle. Sir Gilbert was excessively annoyed at the fact of its being a girl—more annoyed than Fenella had ever seen him during their married life. He had calculated so certainly upon having a son; it did not seem to have entered his head that he might have a daughter.

'Better luck next time, Bertie,' cried Lady Marjoram, who was still a guest at the castle; but her brother did not take the jest in good part.

'My dear, he's as cross as a bear!' she whispered afterwards to Fenella, who could not be put out of conceit with her little girl, although no one seemed to value her but herself; 'but it's always the way with men. They think the world was made for them, and it's a personal insult if they don't get their own way. Marjoram was just the reverse. *He* wanted a daughter, and I had five sons in succession. I can remember his disgusted expression, when he used to exclaim, "*Another* boy! too bad—too bad!" as if *I* could help the young wretches being boys! At last a girl came, and then, of course, he spoilt her. She's the most odious brat of the lot. However, I don't think Bertie will spoil yours—not just yet, at all events.'

'I am afraid not,' said Fenella, with a sigh.

'Don't sigh over it, you muff; it's not *your* fault; and if Bertie begins any more grumbling, just give him a bit of your mind. You're too easy with him, Fenella. He's growing a regular bully! —No, nurse! don't ask me to kiss the baby, *please!* I daresay she's a very nice baby, and everything she ought to be; but, you see, I have nine of my own, and the gilt has somewhat worn off the gingerbread! In fact (not to put too fine a point upon it) the game's played out.'

And without another look at the infant, the lively Countess ran away.

The new-comer was left entirely to the admiration of its mother and nurses, but doubtless it fared none the worse for that.

'And she's come in *February* too,' re-marked Bennett, significantly, to Fenella, as she cradled the little Conroy in her arms; 'that seems as if she was to be a special gift, my lady, doesn't it ?'

This idea seemed to linger in the mind of the young mother, and when next she saw Sir Gilbert she asked him if their little girl might be called Theodora.

' Theodora—Theodora !' he repeated, wrinkling his brows. 'Why Theodora ? It wasn't your mother's name, was it ?'

' Oh no; mamma was called Rosina ! But Theodora, you know, means " the gift of God."'

' Exactly so, though I don't see that this baby is more especially the gift of God than any other baby—do you ?'

Fenella looked down at the child lying on her breast.

'She is such a *comfort* to me!' she answered, as she strained her to her heart.

'I am glad of that, dear,' said her husband, 'and I should like to indulge your fancy in the matter; but being the eldest daughter, I think she ought to be called after my mother, Lady Valeria; and so does Janie.'

'Valeria is such a *fine* name. It doesn't seem to *fit* her!' said Fenella dubiously.

'It is not so long as Theodora, at any rate,' laughed Sir Gilbert; 'however, Valeria, she must be, so I am sure you will not oppose yourself to what I think best.'

She had never done so yet, and was not likely to begin now. The baby was baptized in the name of Valeria, and Fenella soon became reconciled to a matter of so little importance. But when the child was about a month old, a real trial assailed her. Sir Gilbert Conroy was offered the governorship of Sovooranooko, and decided to accept it. The temptation was too great for him. What real sportsman could resist the chance of bagging game in the African forests? Visions of elephants, rhinoceri, hippopotami, gorillas, elands, and buffalo floated rapturously through the baronet's brain, until he was no longer master of himself. He accepted the post without even consulting his wife in the matter, and made immediate arrangements for going up to town and purchasing every sort of weapon and equipment necessary for his expected experiences. Lord Laurence Grantham (as enthusiastic a sportsman as himself) was to accompany him as his private secretary, and much good might Sovooranooko expect to derive from their united services whilst a head of game remained within range of their rifles.

On first hearing the news of her husband's appointment, Fenella naturally supposed she was to accompany him.

' But will Sovooranooko be a good place

to take baby to?' she demanded timidly.
'Do you think the climate will agree with
her, Gilbert?'

'My dear girl, what are you dreaming of?
Drag a baby and suite after me into the
centre of Africa? I'd as soon think of
introducing a gorilla into your London
drawing-room.'

'But how can I leave her behind, so
young as she is?' she asked him.

'I don't wish you to leave her behind.
I should no more think of risking your
health than I should that of the child.
No, my dear Fenella, this is not an expe-
dition for women and children. Grantham
and I shall spend half our time in the
jungle, and what would you do without
society, grilling away on the burning plains
of Sovooranooko? It would kill you both.'

'But if it is so dangerous a climate,
why do you go there, Gilbert?' she exclaimed, with a sudden outburst of affection. 'Why should you leave us for years,
to hold an appointment which you do not

require, and from which you may never return ?'

Sir Gilbert had to consider for a moment why he did do this thing, before he could answer his wife's question.

'Well, the reason, my dear, is obvious. I certainly do not actually require the appointment, nor do I admire the climate ; but still it is a great honour conferred upon me, and my longing to have some sport in Central Africa has always been intense. In my position as governor of Sovooranooko, I shall not only have better opportunities of following the pursuit, but be able to penetrate farther and with greater security than I should otherwise be able to do. But as for my remaining away for *years*, that is nonsense. There is no necessity for me to go at all, and I can resign the appointment whenever I feel inclined.'

'Janie says, when you once get there, it is a question whether you will *ever* come back again,' said Fenella.

' Janie knows nothing about it. We certainly cannot commence following up the large game until a particular season of the year ; but I shall not remain out there a minute longer than I find it pay me to do so. Meanwhile, Fenella, there is no need for you to mope. You will be a great deal with my sister, I hope, when you are in London ; and the autumn you will spend at the sea-side, or wherever pleases you. Perhaps the Marjorams may ask you down to Southfield for Christmas. I am sure they will, if you evince the slightest disposition to join them. But since Dr M'Kenzie advises your going to some warmer place for the next few months, I shall not leave England until I have seen you comfortably settled at Nice, or wherever you like best.'

From the extreme cold of Scotland Fenella had developed a cough after her baby's birth. Had she been an ordinary patient it would have been treated with syrup of squills, but in the position of Sir

Gilbert Conroy's wife the family doctor considered it necessary to prescribe a visit to the south coast to expedite her cure; and, after some deliberation, Hyères in France was chosen for her temporary sojourn.

Sir Gilbert would have had his wife travel with a courier, and a flunky, and a couple of women, and engage the best suite of rooms in the best hotel. He was a man who loved pomp and show, and if there was an ungentlemanly trait in his character, it was his weakness to be thought a very big person, and to have everything belonging to him in equal style. Fenella pleaded hard to be excused the courier and the flunky, for neither of whom she had the slightest use; but she took Bennett and her lady's-maid with her, and permitted her husband to establish them in the hotel at Hyères, and impress the proprietor and attendants with a sense of the importance of Miladi Conroy, and the necessity that she should be supplied with everything that was best and most expensive. And thus, having fulfilled the very letter of the law as a husband and protector, Sir Gilbert gave Fenella un-limited credit at his banker's, and parted with her as carelessly as if he had been running into the country for a fortnight's fishing.

His wife felt very lonely after he was gone—still more so when she heard that he had left England in the Cape steamer, and was on his way to Sovooranooko. She began to wish she had not left Conroy Castle, or that she had asked her sister-in-law to receive her as a guest at Southfield. But the Earl and Countess were paying a round of visits, and she would have been almost as lonely in either of those places as at Hyères. Then her lady's-maid (who had never been a favourite with Fenella) began to give her trouble. She was an independent, free-born Britisher, and not disposed to fall in kindly with any of the ways of 'them

nasty furriners.' She complained of the
food and the accommodation ; she couldn't
'abide' to see the invalids who had come to
Hyères (perhaps only to die) being dragged
about in their wheel-chairs ; and she didn't
understand 'hupper' servants being put to
one side by 'nusses,' and such like—which
being interpreted, meant that the lady's-
maid was jealous of the confidences reposed in Bennett by her mistress.

'*Hif* her la'ship required her services,
would she be good enough to say so? and
hif her la'ship didn't, would she be good
enough to let her go ? '

When it came to this pointed appeal,
Fenella found she could do very much
better without her.

'Do send her away, my dear lady,'
whispered Bennett. 'I can do everything
that you and the baby require ; and she's
always got her ear at the keyhole, listening to every word we say.'

So the lady's-maid (much to her surprise and annoyance) was dismissed from

Lady Conroy's service, and sent back to England; and shortly after her departure Fenella removed from the hotel, and took a lovely little cottage standing in its own garden, on the outskirts of the town, where Bennett, and a *fille de quartier* hired in Hyères, rendered her all the assistance she required.

These may appear to be trifling and unnecessary details, but they exerted a strong influence upon her future conduct. Here, in this solitude, with no society but that of Eliza Bennett and her little infant, Fenella lapsed into very low spirits. Her life had become calm and contented, but it was not sufficiently happy to bear the strain of her own thoughts, without the outward distraction of cheerful company and lively surroundings. Left to herself, she was too apt to dream; and dreaming revealed a state of mind that half frightened her. She was sadly disappointed, too, at Sir Gilbert leaving her for Sovooranooko, although she would not acknowledge it,

even to herself. But she had begun to
lean upon the fact that he was her·hus-
band; to misconstrue the courtesy and
deference (which he would have shown
to any woman) as marks of love for herself, and to deceive her own heart into
the belief that she loved him in return.
And yet he had left her for an indefinite
period, whilst he ran all the risks attendant
on an unhealthy climate and a dangerous
pursuit; and Fenella could not help recog-
nising her true place in his estimation.
She was Lady Conroy, his wife, and the
possible mother of his heir—that was all.
As for the poor little girl in the cradle,
he had not even looked at her before he
went away. She was a female, of no consequence at all in his family tree; that she
was her mother's child gave her no individual claim upon her father's heart.
But the little Valeria (now three months
old) was daily becoming more engaging in
Fenella's eyes, who thought that a lovelier
specimen of babyhood had never existed.

And she was partly right. The infant was unusually large and fat for her age—too much so, indeed, for health, as the sequel proved. For one day, as the little creature was lying, flushed and rosy in her sleep, she was seized (without the slightest warning) with a convulsion, from which she never recovered. Bennett (who had frequently seen infants in fits before) plunged her at once into a warm bath, and held her there until the convulsions had ceased. But when they were over, life was over too. The beautiful baby had closed her blue eyes upon this world for ever, and Bennett was forced to break the intelligence to her mistress. The *fille de quartier* was sent flying into Hyères for a doctor, but he only arrived to confirm the nurse's opinion. The spirit of the little child was gone beyond recall—' if he could be of any other use to Miladi he would be but too happy, but as for *this*,' shrugging his shoulders, ' he was *accomblé* with regret to say it—but no one could help Miladi *here*.'

It was some time before Fenella could be made to believe that her infant was really dead. But when the doctor had departed, and the little body was laid out, stiff and white, upon the bed, her agony was overwhelming.

'There is a curse upon me, Bennett,' she cried, as she fell, sobbing, on her knees beside the corpse. 'God is still angry with me! I shall never be the mother of a living child!'

'No, no! my dear lady; don't say that, for it isn't the truth. Oh, if I only dared to tell you!' said Bennett, with the tears streaming down her own face.

'You cannot tell me anything to give me comfort,' replied Fenella, as she rocked herself to and fro. 'They all leave me; no one stays with me! I believe I am doomed to live and die alone! *What* had I, nurse — *whom* had I—but this little child? and God has taken even her away! Oh! it is cruel —it is *cruel* of Him! He might have left me *one* of them, just to save my heart from breaking !'

The servant, who was almost as upset as her mistress, sat by her side all night long, and never left her for one moment to herself.

On the evening of the next day (according to the custom of that part of the country) Fenella's child was buried, and the little house seemed as if it had died itself—it was so empty and still and forlorn.

Lady Conroy had wept until her sight was dull and her face sodden ; she had paced up and down the room until she had nearly fainted from fatigue and want of nourishment ; but still she could not rest. She moved about incessantly, with dry eyes, but burning cheeks, recalling every incident in her baby's short life which could increase her grief and heighten her despair. At last she made a dart at her blotting-case.

'I cannot write to Sir Gilbert,' she

said, 'until I have heard of his arrival at Sovooranooko; but I must let Lady Marjoram know the news at once. They would never forgive me if I kept them in ignorance of such an event. Though I don't suppose any of them will care if she is alive or dead. No one loved her but myself. My darling little Valeria! my poor lost baby!'

She sat down with the blotting-book in her hand, and burst into a fresh flood of tears. This was the moment Bennett had been watching for. As the tempest of Fenella's grief subsided, she found her faithful dependant close at hand.

'Don't write this evening, my darling child,' she said affectionately; 'you ain't fit for it. Let it be till to-morrow, for there's something as I want to tell you.'

'Tell it me afterwards, dear Bennett. Let me write my letters first,' pleaded Fenella. 'It will do me good to have some occupation. Besides, we must leave this place, nurse. I can't stay here, now

my baby's gone. I should fancy I heard
her voice crying every minute.'

'Yes, yes! my dear lady,' replied
Bennett soothingly; 'and you know as
you can do exactly as you choose in all
things. Only there's something as I
want to tell you, my dear, and I've
wanted to tell it you for months and
months past, only I didn't dare; but the
time's come now, I'm sure, and I don't
feel as if I should do right to keep it
to myself any longer. I think it will be
a comfort to you, and yet how to begin
the story I don't know.'

The woman's manner was so earnest
and yet full of mystery, as she walked to
the door and locked it, lest they should be
interrupted, that Fenella's curiosity was
immediately aroused.

'Nurse, what is it you can have to tell
me that requires so much preparation? Is
it anything to do with poor mamma?'

'Well, it has and it hasn't, Miss
Fenella; and I expect you'll be so sur-

prised, you'll hardly believe as I'm telling you the truth. But you mustn't blame me, my dear, for I can call Heaven to witness as I never did anything in this world but what I thought was for your good.'

'What on earth is it?' cried Fenella, as the blotting-case slid to the ground. 'I begin to be frightened, nurse. Surely it cannot be more bad news for me?'

'No, no, my lamb. I think you'll say as it's good news, and I am sure you will say I am right to tell it you. Do you remember the time, Miss Fenella, when you was so ill at Sainte Pauvrette?'

Lady Conroy shuddered.

'Ah, Bennett, as if I could *ever* forget it! It is the one great black spot in my life.'

'Your mamma told you then, miss, as your baby was dead, and you cried bitterly for it's loss, didn't you?'

The tears streamed afresh down Fenella's face. The old wound had recalled the new.

'Oh yes, I did! My poor wee baby that never saw the light! God might have left me *this* one (mightn't He, nurse?) just to help me to forget the other.'

'And what should you say, my dear,' continued Bennett, as she softly stroked the girl's hand; 'what should you say, now, if I was to tell you as your first baby —the baby that was born at Sainte Pauvrette—was still alive?'

Lady Conroy half sprung from her seat, and stared into the servant's face incredulously.

But my mother — my *mother*,' she panted, 'told me it was born dead—that it never even breathed on entering the world!'

'My mistress didn't tell the truth then, Miss Fenella—God forgive her! That child was born alive, and is living now.'

'But I never saw it, nurse! I never heard it cry!'

'I daresay not, my dear, or you don't

remember it. But you were raving with fever all the time, and the baby was safe in England long before you came to your senses again.'

' But you showed me her grave!' continued Lady Conroy, with eyes wide open with surprise. 'You pointed out a little mound to me in Sainte Pauvrette churchyard, and told me my poor baby lay beneath it, and I left violets and primroses there for her sake.'

' My dear, I did; and I'm not going to deny it. They was your poor mamma's orders, and I obeyed them, as I've obeyed many an order of hers that's laid on my conscience since. But it was untrue, Miss Fenella. I took your dear baby myself to England the very day she was born, and she's living there to this hour. And that's God's truth, my lamb, if I never utter another word on this side the grave!'

Fenella stood still and silent for one moment, as if to try and grasp the truth of this unexpected revelation. Then with a cry of indignation she bounded to her feet.

'And *my mother* did this!' she exclaimed. '*My mother*, who brought me into the world, and knew all that I had suffered! She stepped into the place of God and bereaved me of my child! How did she *dare* to do it?' she went on fiercely, as she confronted Eliza Bennett. 'How did *you* dare to uphold her in such a falsehood? What right had you to conspire together to steal my child from me—*his* child—and leave me to the desolation and despair that followed? How did you *dare* — how did you DARE to do it?'

She paced up and down the room as she spoke, alarming Bennett beyond measure by her heightened colour and rapid utterance.

'Say what you like to me, Miss Fenella,' she replied piteously; 'I daresay I did very wrong, though I acted under orders. But don't go to blame your dear mamma as is a saint in heaven. She did it for the best, my dear; she thought to save you the shame and the distress it might prove in after-years. We talked a deal together about it before we decided what to do, but the little one's been safe and well with my sister Martha ever since, and you'll be able to see her now whenever you like. And oh! do stop walking in that fashion, my dear, for if you fall ill, I shall never forgive myself for having told you; but I thought maybe it might be a comfort for you to hear, now that the other dear baby's gone.'

Fenella stopped short, and flung herself on her knees by the old woman's side.

'It *is* a comfort, dear Bennett,' she said; 'but tell me the truth—don't deceive me any more—is she really alive?'

'She *is* alive, my dear. She's a poor creature, as might be expected, brought up by hand; but she's alive and well.'

'And what is she like, nurse? Oh, tell me what my child is like.'

'She ain't so good-looking as the angel that's gone, Miss Fenella, but I should think she'd take after you when she fills out a bit. She's very backward, poor lamb; she can't say a word, and she's got no use of her legs. But Martha's took every care of her, and couldn't love her better if she were her own.'

'And—and—does Martha know that she belongs to *me*, nurse?' asked Lady Conroy hesitatingly.

'Bless your heart, *no!* Do you think I'd go to pull down the family in *that* way, Miss Fenella? In course not! I said 'twas a child belonging to a friend of my mistress, and they didn't ask no questions. Why should they? They've been paid reg'lar ever since.'

'Who has paid them, Bennett?'

'Well, your dear mamma did up to her death, my lady, and since that your ten-pound note has kept them going till such time as I could make up my mind to tell you the truth.'

'Oh, if I could see her! if I could only see her!' cried Fenella, clasping her hands.

'My dear, I don't see why you shouldn't, and that's why I wanted to tell you my story before you wrote to Lady Marjoram.'

'What has that to do with it, Bennett? I couldn't tell *her*, you know.'

'I should think not! You'll be very soft if you tell any one now. Let the matter rest between you and me, my dear. But ain't it next to a moral certainty as Sir Gilbert will be out in that African place for some years?'

'I believe so. For two or three years, without doubt, unless some accident sends him home.'

'Well, then, Miss Fenella, I'd risk it!'

''Risk what, Bennett?'

'I'd have that baby home in place of the

one that's gone, and trust to his never finding out the difference.'

'Nurse! what are you thinking of? My first baby must be fifteen months old by this time.'

'I know she is, my dear, and of course you couldn't manage it if you was in England, or Sir Gilbert likely to come home soon. But she's a puny little thing, you must be prepared for that; and though you couldn't pass her off now for a baby of three months, I warrant that when she's three years you will be very well able to pass her off as a child of two. And Sir Gilbert is not a gentleman to fuss over children, you know. He'll never put his foot in the nursery if he can help it. I believe you might bring up half-a-dozen there without his being any the wiser.'

'Lady Marjoram?' faltered Fenella.

'I'll manage the Countess, my dear. You see, if you fall in with my notion, you must say the baby's delicate, and leave her with me when you go to London for the season. Lady Marjoram will never trouble you with any questions about her.'

'Oh, if I *could*—if I only could!' cried the mother, with a new hope beaming in her eyes. 'My poor neglected baby! my poor fatherless lamb! I *must* have her back again.'

'It would do my heart good to see her in your arms,' said Bennett, 'for it smites me every time I go to Ines-cedwyn and look at the poor little thing. For 'tain't *her* fault, you see, Miss Fenella; *she* ain't the one to blame, pretty dear; and it seems terrible hard she should grow up without any one to love her as she has a claim to, and no more knowledge than can be got in Ines-cedwyn.'

'She never shall!' exclaimed Lady Conroy; 'I will claim her and look after her, even if I am not able to bring her up by my side. Bennett! Bennett!' she continued, in a lower voice, as she pulled the old woman's face close down to her own, 'tell me, *dear* Bennett, is she at all like *him?*'

'Lor'! Miss Fenella, why should you go to ask me such a thing? I'm sure I don't know, my dear, and I hopes, for your sake, as she's not, for you ought to have forgotten all about him long and long ago.'

Lady Conroy hid her face in the servant's bosom.

'Oh yes! I know I *ought*, and I think I have too (nearly, that is to say), only this stirs it up, you see, Bennett—it stirs it up.'

'But has it comforted you, my dear lady, or have I made matters worse by my chattering?'

'No, no! May God Almighty bless you, Bennett, for having told me that my baby lives. It has comforted me as nothing else in this world could have done. It has almost reconciled me to giving back the other one to Heaven.

CHAPTER VIII.

THE INDISSOLUBLE LINK.

'Child of my love! essence of all things fair,
    Sweet outcome of my happy, hopeful youth,
    Sweet mem'ry of thy father's passionate truth,
Come nearer; let me feel that thou art there.
Give me thy hand—'twas thus I held his own;
Look in my eyes—'twas thus I gaz'd in his;
Kiss me for him—one fervent, long-drawn kiss—
And tell me that we part for earth alone.'

HOW will it be possible to adequately describe Fenella's feelings at this juncture, so as to make those who read of them judge her leniently? No *man* could do it; no man could even understand the emotions that passed through her mind, or enter into the passion that actuated her conduct.

A man must stand on one side and be
dumb. And neither could a woman, unless she had been a mother, and received
back her child, as it were, from the dead;
even a woman must have passed through
similar circumstances before she could
comprehend the difficult position in which
Fenella was placed. Picture her wild surprise on hearing that the child of her love
—the child of the man whom she could not
forget—still lived, and was dependent on
her; that somewhere in this wide world
it stretched tiny arms to the empty air,
yearning for a mother's tenderness; and
then think of the impossibility of her
telling the secret to any one—of the
impossibility of her having the infant
with her at all unless she stooped to a
deception which seemed innocent beside
the crime of disowning it. Once made
aware of its existence, Fenella could not
close her eyes to her responsibility. She
could not have done it under any circumstances, for her heart was that of a true

mother, and she would have gone forth
into the world, if needful, with her baby
in her arms, and supported it by the
most menial of labour, sooner than have
confided it any longer to the care of
strangers.

But there was another motive working
in her breast, a motive for which the
world (who embraces coroneted cour-
tesans) will be the most ready to condemn
her,—she loved the father of her child
with every fibre of her heart. It was
her greatest sin, this impossibility to be
faithless and forget. Let it be written
down against her. This is not the history of a saint. It only professes to be
the record of an erring woman's life.

But Fenella did not intend at first to
follow Bennett's suggestion in all its
details. It is questionable, indeed, if she
ever intended to do so, for she was
true by nature (as has already been
pointed out), and it was only the greater
passion fighting against the lesser that

made her untrue to her nature now. It is the same with all of us when brought face to face with the greatest difficulties of our lives—the master-passion (whichever it may be) prevails. And Fenella's master-passion—whether it demonstrated itself in one phase or another—was love.

When the wonder and the surprise of the revelation had somewhat subsided—when she had heard every detail that the nurse could give her of the circumstances under which her infant had been placed in the charge of Martha Bennett, and was thoroughly convinced that there was a living being dependent upon her alone for care and support and affection in the future, then all the mother's love came welling forth, and Fenella felt as if she could not rest until she held her child in her arms.

Bennett did not fail to improve the occasion. Her conscience had sorely upbraided her for taking part in the deception even from the beginning, but she had

been a tool in the hands of Mrs Barrington, and had simply done as her mistress
commanded her.   But the spell was
broken now; the magnetic chain which
the frivolous woman of fashion seemed to
have woven about the will of her dependant was snapt in two, and Eliza Bennett
could once more think and speak for herself.   She impressed the truth on Lady
Conroy that, if she was ever to act in the
matter, it must be then; that next year,
even next month, might be too late; and
that it would give her incalculable trouble,
and the child incalculable disadvantages
(not only now, but in the future), if she
were not brought up by her side.

'Just think what she may be, fifteen or
twenty years hence, my lady.   Why, the
very thought makes me shudder!   Even
if you was to give her the best of homes
and education, where is she to go when
she's a grown lady?—for a lady she is, my
dear, and nothing can't unmake her that.
And for my part, it seems a moral duty to

me that you should have her home; and, if I may make so bold as to say it, God Almighty seems to have paved the way for you Himself.'

'I intend to reclaim her, Bennett; don't have any fear of that. Do you think I could be so cruel and cowardly as to leave my own little child, that I brought into the world, to grow up without knowing that I am her mother?' exclaimed Fenella. 'Oh no! it is only the *means* of doing it that perplexes me. It can never be justifiable to deceive, you know. And if they should ever find it out—'

'Well, my dear, I shouldn't worry myself about that matter now; and you can do as you think best with respect to Sir Gilbert afterwards. There can never be no call for you to tell Lady Marjoram, surely.'

'Oh no, no!'

'Take a week or two to think over it,' suggested the servant; 'second thoughts is always best. And meanwhile I can fetch the little one, that you may have a look at her.'

Fenella's eyes sparkled with a sudden joy.

' But when, Bennett—*when ?* How soon can you go ? '

' You won't have her *here*, Miss Fenella,' said the woman dubiously.

' I'll do just what you think best.'

' I'd like you to move farther on, my dear—to some place where you are not likely to meet any of your fine friends ; and then when your settled, I'll go over quietly and bring the child back with me.'

' We will go to St Pré,' said Lady Conroy ; ' there is no one there at this time of the year.'

She was burning with anxiety to clasp her baby in her arms. She would have stripped herself of every earthly possession to attain her object. She could think of nothing else until it was accomplished.

Yet the time which Fenella passed alone in the little *auberge* of St Pré, during the

two or three days that her servant was
necessarily absent in England, was one of
great perplexity to her. A dozen plans
for telling the truth, and yet keeping her
first-born by her side, darted into her mind,
and had to be as summarily rejected. Her
husband knew every particular of her former history—of *that* she felt certain—it
had never entered her head for a moment
that it could be otherwise ; but, of course,
Mrs Barrington had told him the same
falsehood she did to herself, and he believed
the baby to be dead. *What* would he say
if he were told it lived ? Would he not
order her never to see it again, never to
speak of it—to bury the fact of its existence in oblivion, as he had desired her to
bury the remembrance of its birth ? And
Fenella felt this was what she could not do.
A chord had been struck in her breast
which vibrated through her whole body.
Her child lived ! The life that was one
with hers had not been quenched, and
whilst it existed they must exist together.

Yet she could not make up her mind what
to do, and she put the question from her
as something to be settled in the future.
But she did not write to announce the
death of little Valeria to Lady Marjoram,
and so the first thread was woven of the net
in which her life was to become entangled.

On the evening on which she had
been led to expect Bennett back again
from Ines-cedwyn, Lady Conroy behaved
like a wild creature.   Her suspense, her
agitation, her anxiety were so extreme,
that she was compelled to go and lock
herself into her own room, that she might
be able to pace the floor, and laugh, and
cry, and talk to herself, as she felt inclined,
without the fear of making the inmates of
the *auberge* say she had gone mad.   At
last, after hours of restless expectation,
Fenella heard a bustle on the stairs,
accompanied by a fretful cry.   She threw
open her bedroom door, and stood panting
on the threshold.

'Give her to me!' she cried impetu-

ously, as Bennett approached with a bundle
in her arms.

'Oh, my lady, be careful! you'll frighten
the child to death.'

But Fenella was not in a condition to
listen to any advice. She hastily tore open
the shawl that enveloped the infant, and met
the gaze of two startled blue eyes, shaded by
dark lashes; a little white face, hardly bigger
than that of the child she had just lost, surrounded by rings of silky brown hair; and a
sad drooping mouth that had just puckered
itself up for another cry. She pounced upon
the baby like a tigress on its prey, and
clasped her vehemently to her bosom.

'Take care, my dear; pray take care,'
repeated the servant fearfully. 'Don't forget she's just come off a long journey, and
everything is strange to her.'

But the mother had got the child's face
close to her own; she saw nothing but the
child—she heard nothing but the throbbing
of her own heart beneath which God had
called it into being.

'*Baby*,' she murmured, in a soft, tremulous voice; 'baby, do you know I am your mother?'

The sweet pathos in her tones attracted the little one's attention. She had just been going to cry, but she thought better of it, and smiled instead.

'She *knows* me!' Fenella cried triumphantly. 'She recognises me, nurse. She sees something in my face she has been waiting for.'

'Bless her heart!' said Eliza Bennett, with the stereotyped nursery benediction, 'she's been good as gold all the way coming over, and Martha was finely put out parting with her, I can tell you; but I said as her mamma had come back from the Injies, and wanted to look after her herself. And I give her the money you sent, my dear, and she considered it most handsome, and she hopes that the child's things (such as they are) will be found in decent order; but, of course, it's little she's been able to do for her that way, for what your dear mamma paid her, though ample, didn't leave much and above over for clothes. But we'll soon put that to rights, won't we, my lady? It'll be quite a pleasure to me to dress the little dear in decent things. But she is a rare little one— ain't she now?'

Bennett might have gone on talking till doomsday, for Fenella was not listening to a word she said. Her eyes, dim with unshed tears, were riveted upon the child, who lay in her arms, passive and contented, as if she knew where she had got to. Suddenly the blue eyes glistened, the tiny fingers were stretched upward, and in another moment had firmly grasped a gold locket which had escaped from the bosom of Fenella's dress. The last pledge that Geoffrey Doyne had given her, in token of his un- alterable fidelity, lay in the hands of his child. At that sight Lady Conroy's tears fell like rain. She turned her face aside, and hid it in the cushion of the sofa upon which she was seated.

'You have been unfaithful to me,' she murmured inwardly ; 'you left me without a thought whether I might not be destroyed, body and soul, by your desertion ; but I will not desert your child. Whatever may happen to me in consequence—whatever I may lose, or give up, or have to resign, I pledge myself here to redeem as much of *my* past as is possible to me, by devoting the rest of my life to the life you created. O Geoffrey ! Geoffrey ! why did you not take mine before you laid this burden on my soul ? '

Bennett perceived that Fenella was weeping, and came at once to the rescue.

'Now, my lady, please, we mustn't have anything of this sort.   I shall be sorry I've brought the baby over here, if she's to be a misery to you instead of a comfort.   Lor' ! what has she got now ?

That there nasty locket! I thought there
was something of that kind in the wind.
Now, my little dear, you please to give
that up, and come to Bennett. 'Twould
have been a deal better for your poor
mamma if she'd never seen the trumpery
thing, nor the one as give it to her
neither. Come, my lady, let me take her,
and you rest yourself on the sofa, whilst
I feed her and put her to bed. She'll
sleep without rocking to-night, I warrant.'

But Fenella would not be parted from
her new-found treasure. Together the
women undressed and washed the infant,
and put it to sleep in the nurse's bed.
And late that night, when the inmates
of the little hotel had long retired, and
Eliza Bennett thought that her mistress
too was wrapt in slumber, a white-robed
figure stole softly to her side, and a low
voice whispered,—

'Is she sleeping, nurse? Has she
taken her food? Are you sure she is
quite comfortable and well?'

'Bless you, yes! my lady. The dear child's sleeping like an angel! Just look at her little face upon the piller. Ain't she like a little wax doll—the pretty dear! But do go back to your bed, Miss Fenella, for you'll get your death of cold standing about these nasty painted boards.'

'I'll go back directly, nurse; but couldn't you bring her and lay her by my side? I think I could go to sleep if I knew that she was there.

'Lor'! my dear, you'd never rest with a baby in your bed. It's terrible, till you're used to them.'

'I think I could—and I would like to try; do wrap a shawl round her and bring her to me. You don't know how my heart does ache! I think if I had my baby next it, it would be a little comfort to me.'

Bennett did not attempt any further remonstrance, but lifting up the sleeping child, carried it into the next room and laid it by its mother's side. And when she crept in again towards the early morn-

ing, to see how they both fared, she found
them in the same position and fast asleep,
the infant's tiny face nestled in Fenella's
bosom. The servant stood and gazed at
them until her eyes filled with tears.

'Well,' she thought to herself, 'if to
bring them two together is a sin, may
God forgive me! but I can't see it. Poor
little mite! don't she look as if she'd got
home at last? And my sweet young lady,
too, is dreaming a happy dream with that
smile upon her lips. May God bless 'em
both! And if any harm comes of it, I'll
work to keep 'em to my life's end.'

And Fenella too, with this new legiti-
mate love awakened in her bosom at the
very moment when it felt so empty and
so cold, was ready to resign the world
itself, if necessary, sooner than give up
her child again. It seemed to her as if
she had never really known what it was
to be a mother until she clasped her in
her arms, and before she had regained
possession of her for a week her infant

had become her idol. She could not
bear her to go out of her sight; she
was always in terror lest some ill should
happen to her; and she spent her
days in studying the tiny features, and
watching the development of the tardily
awakening intellect. She was scarcely
ever out of her mother's arms; day after
day Fenella's tall, lithe figure might be
seen traversing the byroads and field
paths around St Pré, with the fragile
baby clasped to her breast; and the affection of the English lady for her little
child was the observation of every one.
And yet Fenella was not happy. In her
case the saying, ' *Ce n'est que le premier pas
qui coute,*' was eminently true. In delay-
ing to write and announce the death of
Sir Gilbert's child to Lady Marjoram, she
had taken that first step which she would
never be able to retrace; and as day
succeeded day, and the time drew near
for her return to London, she felt that
she must adopt Bennett's suggestion and

keep her own counsel, whether she wished it or not, for there was no possibility of disclosing the truth at that date.

When May arrived she parted from her child with many tears, and leaving it at St Pré under the charge of her nurse and a French *bonne*, travelled to England with her lady's - maid (a new acquisition imported from Paris) to spend the London season under the wing of her sister-in-law.

Lady Marjoram was delighted to receive Lady Conroy, and equally delighted to hear that she had left the baby behind her.

'My dear, how sensible and nice you are! One would believe you were eight-and-twenty instead of eighteen. I can't tell you how I have been dreading the advent of your nursery brigade—not, of course, that they could make any difference to me with my terrible tribe, only I was afraid you'd be running upstairs to see if the little animal was dead or alive twenty times a-day, and wanting to stuff it, with its nurse, on the back seat of the carriage whenever we drove in the park, and all that sort of thing. So interesting you know, my dear, and so abominably disagreeable!'

'I am afraid you must have a very small idea of my common sense, Janie,' replied Fenella, colouring. 'I confess I was very sorry to leave my little girl behind me, but I thought it best for her—particularly as we shall be out, I suppose, day and night.'

'Indeed, we shall, Fenella. This promises to be the gayest season we have had for years. My engagement list is something terrible to look at already. By the way, the Culletons are going to have a series of *tableaux vivants* and private theatricals at Fotheringay House in June and July, and I have promised faithfully that you will assist them. They want the loan of your voice, too, for some amateur concerts. I hope

you have not neglected your singing
lately ?'

'No; I have had a piano wherever I
went, and practised assiduously, and I
intend to take another course of lessons
from Signor Possetrina. By the way,
Janie, I have not yet shown you Gilbert's
last letter. He seems quite delighted
with Sovooranooko, and talks of having
me out there next year to judge of it
for myself.'

'Don't you believe a word of that, my
dear ; it's only a sop for Cerberus. Bertie
has no more idea of having you out to
Sovooranooko than of coming home himself. We had a letter from Lord Laurence
by last mail, and he says Bertie is mad
to get into the interior, and already or-
ganising a shooting party to start as
soon as the cool weather commences.
He has got the Englishman's mania on
him to "kill something," Fenella, and
the best thing you can do is to let him
tire himself out. He'll get a grab from

a lion or a squeeze from a bear some day, and come crying home to you to kiss the place and make it well; but he won't come before. And what should you want to go out to that horrid place for—to lose your complexion and your hair, and perhaps get the yellow fever, or some pleasantry of that sort? Don't you be so silly. You had better stay at home with the baby than do that.'

'Oh yes! I don't want to leave my baby,' cried the mother, with a sudden thrill.

'Well, you couldn't take her with you, so let's talk no more about it. Besides, it is time we went to dress. We have a concert at the Duke of Doldrum's at two.'

The next three months were spent by Fenella in a round of dissipation, during which she distinguished herself in theatricals and at concerts, and heard her talents talked of as much as her beauty had been the year before.

But her heart and all her thoughts were at St Pré. She required *bulletins* to be sent her daily of the health and well-doing of her child, and she bought every dainty little garment or expensive toy she could light upon, to decorate the body, or amuse the mind, of her absent baby.

Lady Marjoram noticed this almost feverish anxiety and restlessness on the part of her sister-in-law concerning her child, and laughed at it. 'It was very becoming,' she said patronisingly, and just as it ought to be, she wished she could get up the same sort of excitement about her own brats. It gave one such a pretty flush to be anxious, and one's eyes looked so quick and bright about the time that the post was expected.

But for all that, Lady Marjoram did not quite believe in the genuineness of Fenella's concern, and she could no more have entered into her real feelings respecting her child than she could sympathise

with Sir Gilbert's exultation at bringing
down an elephant.   The one sensation
was as much a sealed book to her as the
other.   However, as soon as the season
was over, Lady Conroy flew to the side
of her child again, and shed tears of real
joy, because it held out arms of welcome
as soon as it recognised her.

The Earl and Countess of Marjoram
were bound for Norway that year, and as
soon as they had left England, Fenella
brought her little party over, and established them in a lovely Devonshire village
by the sea, where she spent all her days
upon the beach with the little Valeria in
her arms.   For the infant who had been
unbaptized when restored to its mother,
had of course to be called by the name of
the one whose place she assumed.

And here it was, whilst yielding herself
up to the softening influence which nature
generally exerts on a mind fitted to perceive and appreciate her beauties, and
whilst watching the daily growing resem-

blance to her father in the face of her little
child, that Fenella began to have gentler
and more generous thoughts of Geoffrey
Doyne. For since the day on which she received the shock of hearing of his marriage,
the remembrance of him had been fraught
with torture to her. He had never come
into her mind but to suggest something
that was most cruel and heartless and
untrue. She had tried to shut out the
memory even of the time she knew him,
as of some horrible dream that to dwell
upon would madden her. But now, as
little Valeria's baby lips met hers, as she
watched her toddle feebly from one spot
to another, as she heard her faltering
tongue trying to frame the syllables
of '*mother*,' the child's angel whispered to her thoughts of forgiveness
and of mercy, and from the child's eyes
there beamed a look that softened her
recollection of the past.

In fancy, Fenella saw again the flowery
landslip, strewn with fallen petals—fallen

ike her hopes ! she saw the golden sands, the ruined bungalow, the stretch of placid sea, and blue unclouded sky ; and then above, beyond them all, in beauty and in pleasantness, the smile, the look, the tones of Geoffrey Doyne. And she began to make excuses for him—she, who had called him (and justly) by all sorts of hard and ugly names, whose life had been ruined by his desertion— she began to wonder if some dark mystery might not lie at the bottom of his apparent cruelty; whether he could have been told falsehoods of her, or been forced into that marriage that broke her heart ; whether he might not believe that she was dead, or had refused ever to see or speak to him again.   A hundred reasons, all equally vague and improbable, floated through Fenella's mind as she attempted, in her loving generosity, to account for as das- tardly a piece of cruelty as ever a man employed to wreck a woman's life.

She could not satisfy herself.   Her own

nature was too true to accept any excuse
for his conduct, still less for the silence
which preceded and followed it ; yet she
tried so hard, '*for baby's sake*,' she would
say to herself with quivering lips, to make
out the father of her child less undeserv-
ing than he was.

But often (after Fenella had been thinking thus for hours) she would catch her
infant in her arms and sob over it in so
piteous a manner, that the little creature
would weep with terror. And then Fenella would soothe it, and kiss it, and sing
to it, until it smiled again, and whisper
in its ear that its mother would always
love it for its father's sake, although he
had trampled on her heart as if it had
been the ground beneath his feet.

Meanwhile, the little Valeria grew
strong and fat, but still remained so tiny
that Bennett's prophecies concerning her
apparent age seemed likely to be veri-
fied, and when the second London season
dawned upon the world, Fenella ventured

to send her with her nurses up to Conroy Castle, where she remained until her
mother could rejoin her.

'Really, Fenella,' exclaimed Lady Marjoram, 'you are getting too absurdly
domestic! Why should you go and
bury yourself all alone in Scotland
with that child? Why cannot you
spend the autumn at Southfield with
us? I shall be horribly dull without
you.'

'I thought, Janie, that as I had not
been at the castle all last year, and
Gilbert talks of returning in the spring,
he might consider it my duty to go and
look after the place a little.'

'My dear girl, what rubbish! Who
do you suppose looked after it all the
years before he met you? Bertie was
never there, except for the shooting. He
was better employed elsewhere, I can tell
you. Now, do come down to Southfield
with me! It will be a perfect charity.
And send for the child and nurses to

join you there, as I know you will not
come without her.'

'No, I will not come without her,'
replied Fenella, smiling ; and so Bennett
was written to, and in due course appeared with her baby and her *aide-de-
camp* at Southfield.

'And now, pray let us see this wonderful baby,' exclaimed the Countess, on the
first day as they sat together after dinner.
'Your devotion to her is so extraordinary
that it has excited my curiosity. I expect
a *rara avis.* Give your orders, Fenella,
for Bennett to bring the young lady down
to dessert.'

Lady Conroy looked uneasy.

'I think you had better not see her
now,' she said ; 'you don't like children,
and she is very shy with strangers, and
will most likely cry.'

'Never mind ! if she cries, we'll send
her back again,' replied Lady Marjoram,
who always liked to have her own way.
'I think it is quite time I made the

acquaintance of my niece. Let me see! How old is she?'

'Eighteen months,' said Fenella, in a low voice.

'Quite grown up, I declare,' laughed her sister-in-law. 'Send for her at once. The girls are so precocious now-a-days, that at this rate she will be married before I see her.'

The order was given, and in a few minutes a tap was heard upon the dining-room door, and Bennett entering, set down with much pride upon the carpet a tiny creature, dressed in lace and ribbons, of about two feet high, who stood the centre of attraction, looking with scared and wistful eyes upon the strangers.

'Baby!' said Fenella, in her sweet, low voice.

The little figure fluttered like a blue-and-white butterfly, and then with a cry of pleasure tottered to her mother's side, and laid her curly head against her knee. Fenella lifted her in her arms, and pressed her glowing face in the folds of the infant's frock.

'What a little fairy,' cried the Countess. 'She looks as if she had just stepped, ready dressed, out of the Soho Bazaar! Marjoram! why don't my children make a rush at me like that? Why do they always hang back and stick their fingers in their mouths, and their heads in the nurse's apron? Look at that child! stroking Fenella's face like a grown being! I should get quite fond of a baby if it showed as much sense as that.'

'She has always been with me,' said Fenella ingenuously.

'That's it,' acquiesced the Earl. 'Lady Conroy has nursed her child, and you leave yours to a set of hirelings.'

'Hold your tongue, Marjoram! you don't know anything about it. How old did you say she was, Fenella? Can she talk?'

'Very little, Janie. She can only say "mother," and "father," and "Bennie."'

'And whom does she resemble? Turn her face round, my dear, that I may see it,' continued Lady Marjoram.

Fenella grew crimson.

'They say she is very like *me*,' she answered, with a rapidly beating heart.

'Not a bit of it,' cried the Countess. 'She's the very image of Bertie! The hair's a trifle darker, perhaps, but that is the only difference I can see. I shall tell him so in my next letter. Well, Bennett, you can take Miss Conroy away now if you like, and I think she is a very fine little girl for her age, and does you a great deal of credit.'

'Thank you, my lady,' replied the servant, as she disengaged the clinging arms from about her mistress's neck, and conveyed little Valeria out of sight again.

After that interview Fenella's heart grew secure, and she took her child about with her wherever she went.

Since she had passed the crucible of

Lady Marjoram's scrutiny, she considered that all risk of discovery was over; and so much does custom become our second nature, that at times Fenella almost forgot what she had done, and detected herself waking with a start, to remember that Valeria was not Sir Gilbert Conroy's child. That is, she contrived to lull her uneasy conscience to sleep respecting the deception she had practised, so long as it seemed to concern no one but herself. But the day arrived when the person who had been most injured by the transaction reappeared upon the scene, and from that moment the heart of Fenella reasserted itself, and refused to be quieted by any specious arguments that tried to make a wrong thing look as if it were right.

With the return of spring came Sir Gilbert Conroy from Sovooranooko. He had not resigned his appointment, but he required change of air and relaxation, and had procured so many months' leave to England in consequence. He came back

accompanied by his private secretary, and
laden with the spoils of the chase, in excellent humour with the world, his wife,
himself, and everybody belonging to him.
But with the first kiss of welcome he
bestowed upon her, all Fenella's fancied
serenity fled like a dream, and for the
first time she saw what she had done in
its true light.

END OF VOL. II.

COLSTON AND SON, PRINTERS, EDINBURGH.

www.ingramcontent.com/pod-product-compliance
Lightning Source LLC
Chambersburg PA
CBHW060521030726
47498CB00004B/1027